COWGIRL FALLIN' FOR THE SINGLE DAD

BRIDES OF MILLER RANCH, N.M. BOOK 1

NATALIE DEAN

DEDICATION

*I'd like to dedicate this book to YOU! The readers of my books.
Without your interest in reading these heartwarming stories of love,
I wouldn't have made it this far. So thank you so much for taking
the time to read any and hopefully all of my books.*

*And I can't leave out my wonderful mother, son, sister, and Auntie.
I love you all, and thank you for helping me make this happen.*

Most of all, I thank God for blessing me on this endeavor.

*AND... I've got a special team of advance readers who are always so
helpful in pointing out any last minute corrections that need to be
made. I'm so thankful to those of you who are so helpful!*

OTHER BOOKS BY NATALIE DEAN

CONTEMPORARY ROMANCE

Miller Family Saga

BROTHERS OF MILLER RANCH

Miller Family Saga Series 1

Her Second Chance Cowboy

Saving Her Cowboy

Her Rival Cowboy

Her Fake-Fiance Cowboy Protector

Taming Her Cowboy Billionaire

Brothers of Miller Ranch Complete Collection

MILLER BROTHERS OF TEXAS

Miller Family Saga Series 2

The New Cowboy at Miller Ranch Prologue

Humbling Her Cowboy

In Debt to the Cowboy

The Cowboy Falls for the Veterinarian

Almost Fired by the Cowboy

Faking a Date with Her Cowboy Boss

Miller Brothers of Texas Complete Collection

BRIDES OF MILLER RANCH, N.M.

Copper Creek Romances Series 2

Making a Cowgirl

Marrying a Cowgirl

Christmas with a Cowgirl

Trusting a Cowgirl

Dating a Cowgirl

Catching a Cowgirl

Loving a Cowgirl

Marrying a Cowboy

Callahans of Copper Creek Complete Collection

KEAGANS OF COPPER CREEK

Copper Creek Romances Series 3

Some Cowboys are Off-Limits

Some Cowgirls Love Single Dads

Some Cowboys are Infuriating

Some Cowboys Don't Like City Girls

Some Cowboys Heal Broken Hearts

Some Cowgirls are Worth Protecting

Some Cowboys are Just Friends (Coming August 2024)

Though I try to keep this list updated in each book, you may also visit my website nataliedeanauthor.com for the most up to date information on my book list.

CONTENTS

1

Charity

"Aw, come off it, the date couldn't have gone *that* bad."

"Nah, I'm telling you, Charity, I can sense it. That guy totally googled me. I could practically smell it on him that he was more interested in our money than me."

Charity rolled her eyes at the ridiculous statement. "Cass, if you keep accusing everyone of being after our money, I'm sure eventually you'll be right."

"I don't understand how you can be so hopeful. Especially considering... you know."

Charity felt her stomach twist. "Just because I haven't had a ton of luck doesn't mean that you're going to run into the same thing, you know."

There was silence on the other side for a little while, the phone only picking up the sound of the blinker. An inconvenience of using the car's built-in Bluetooth, but Charity and all of her siblings were incredibly good about hands-free driving. It had been one of Mama's soapboxes that she liked to get on from time to time, and even after so long without her, that lesson had stuck with the entire brood.

"...but I *don't* know that, Charity. And that's why this whole dating thing is a waste of time."

Guilt coiled in Charity, heavy and thick. Her younger sister was clearly scared to date after seeing the train wreck of Charity's marriage. She was supposed to lead by example, and instead, she'd traumatized at least one of her siblings. Even her brother Charlie had been different when he'd come home from college and seen her marriage in tatters, going from a flirtatious skirt-chaser to someone completely uninterested in the fairer sex at all.

"Cass, you have to listen to me, okay?"

"Uh-oh, that's your big sister voice."

"You bet it is—because I'm about to say something important. Cassidy Miller, you are going to be thirty soon and are one of the hottest, most eligible women in half the state's radius. You have had men pining over you since you were eighteen, and probably a few more years before that considering the knuckle-busters I used to get in with the creeps around the bar.

"I understand and respect you being cautious, I do. But all men aren't going to be like my ex. In fact, *most* men won't be like my ex. I won't pretend like there aren't plenty of people around who want a slice of the Miller pie, but you have to stop assuming and give guys a chance."

Silence again on the other side, but Charity wasn't overly worried about it. Her next-youngest sister had always been a firebrand. She was two years younger than Charity, but everyone had always said they were two peas in a pod. Fiery, determined, and pretty much unstoppable.

"You're right," Cass said with a sigh. "I just... I guess I'll try to work on it. You know, for being an old lady, you're not that bad of a big sister."

Charity laughed. There was her lil' sis. "Hey, now listen here, you ungrateful—"

But Cass was already yelling at someone else before Charity could finish. "Hey! What are you—"

A violent booming sound forced its way through the phone speaker, followed by a horrific shriek. Noise after noise grated into Charity's ears in tinny drafts, louder than all of her thoughts and seeming to make her entire mind blink out.

It seemed to last forever, a whole symphony of destructive sounds, but it probably could only have been a few minutes.

"Cass! Cassidy Miller, can you hear me? This better not be some sort of joke!"

No response from her sister.

"Cass!?" she called again, knowing her voice was shrill.

She heard a groan, so tiny, so weak that it was barely there at all, then a crackle and the line went dead. Horror filling her heart, she felt her phone slip through her fingers, clattering to the porch below her feet.

Everything was spinning, everything was *screaming* at her, and Charity sucked in a long, deep breath. It didn't help, not really, but it gave her enough fuel to open her mouth and yell.

"*PAPA!*"

2

––––––––––

Charity

"Here, let me just adjust—"

"I'm *fine*," Cass said, her lips pulling back on her pale face in an expression that could only be called a snarl.

Charity froze in the middle of bending down to adjust the footrest for her sister, giving Cass a steady look.

That seemed to be what she needed because Cass grimaced. "Sorry. But I'm fine. Just get me inside."

"Of course. Time to break in the ramp me n' Papa built, I guess."

"Uh-huh." Cass's response was taciturn and weary, but Charity couldn't exactly blame her. Although they were all excited that the second eldest sister of their family had been cleared to go home from the hospital, it wasn't exactly an easy road they had all traveled together.

Charity squeezed her eyes shut for a moment, trying not to remember that night, how she and Papa had called the police, reporting that *something* had happened. Cass was too far away for Charity to go find her, so they had to just wait. The police arrived hours later to tell them that Cass had been in an accident.

An accident.

Such a simple word for the horror that had happened. Charity didn't think she would ever get those sounds out of her head, how the phone's speaker had been overloaded with the shriek of metal twisting in on itself. And she wasn't even the one *in* the accident.

No, that was just Cass.

It had been... close, to put it mildly. There were several times in the week after where they almost lost her. First just due to the sheer trauma and blood loss since it took them so long to free her from the wreck, and then due to a wicked and virulent infection. Charity had always thought that hospitals were supposed to be *clean*, where people went to get rid of infections, not get them, but she'd learned a lot in the two and a half months since the accident.

Like, for example, how to build a wheelchair ramp up to their family home.

They weren't poor, by any means, and if it was out of her depth, Charity would have had no problem hiring a contractor. But building the ramp and handrails and things herself made her feel slightly less powerless, and frankly she needed all the distraction she could get.

Their whole family did, really. They'd already lost their mother, losing Cass on top of that would have been... too much. Just too much.

"How am I supposed to get up to my room?" Cass asked quietly once she was inside, a shadow of her former self.

Charity wasn't under any illusions about how much pain her sister had been in. Broken bones had needed to be reset, and her brain had been swollen and angry from slamming against the back of her skull, then the front of it, before rattling around for a while. Then there was the compression to her spine, the whiplash, and the fact that her femur had been broken in two different places.

And that wasn't counting the shrapnel, or the airbag burns.

Thinking about it made Charity's stomach twist and she did her best to paste on a carefree smile as she answered her sister.

"You're not going to believe this, but we hired a company and put a lift in!"

"A lift?"

Charity nodded, pushing her sister through the main hall and around the staircase that led to the upper floors.

As a part of the extended Miller family, they had plenty of money, but Charity was aware that her family's home was right humble compared to the Montana Millers and basically a shack compared to the Texas Millers. Seeing as how they had two floors plus a finished basement and attic, there was more than enough room for Charity, her four siblings and their Papa.

Not that their house was tiny by any means. Somewhere along the lines of what was apparently called "cottagecore," it was big enough for them to never feel cramped but small enough so that it wasn't empty feeling. Charity had only been to her cousins' mansion once, but the whole place gave her the willies. Like no one was supposed to live there and it was only for display purposes.

"Oh wow," Cass said as they rounded the corner to the small, wheelchair-friendly lift that they had paid a pretty penny to put in.

At first they had intended to give Cass a temporary room on the main floor, maybe changing out their modest personal library or hang out room, but when the doctor said she could have two or so years of recovery to regain all of her motor function, they'd decided that they weren't going to exile Cass from the rest of the family for that long.

"You guys *do* know that I'm going to get better, right? And then this lift will be useless."

"I don't know about useless. My knees have been loving this in my old age."

"Charity, you're thirty-two."

"Oh, is that it? Doesn't feel that way sometimes."

Cass huffed a weak sort of laugh. It wasn't anything like how she used to be, but Charity understood. Her sister *hated* being sick and would become a real grouch every time she had a cold or the flu. What she was going through was definitely more serious than that, and Charity could tell her younger sister was trying not to take it out on them.

Trying, but not always succeeding. But Charity let her sister barb at her whenever she needed. After all, Charity was the oldest and supposed to protect her siblings. Sure, maybe they were all grown, but that didn't matter to her. Ever since Mama had passed, it had been her job to help Papa and her siblings.

He had never asked her to do that, of course. In fact, Papa had always tried to convince her to do things for herself and would readily agree to almost any preteen activity if it meant she was taking the time to be a kid. He always told her that he didn't want her to become a third parent, and the only responsibilities she had was to be happy, healthy, and kind. Charity had always understood *why* he'd said that—because he cared for her and didn't want to see her take on the burdens of an adult. But what he never quite seemed to get was that it was never an *obligation* for her.

From the age that Charity was old enough to have her own thoughts, she'd been fiercely protective of those closest to her. She remembered when her mother had gotten cut while washing the dishes and how she'd hugged her and peppered Mama's face with kisses until she was sure her mom wasn't in pain anymore. She also remembered employing a similar kissing strategy when Cass was somewhere around two and had fallen, scraping her knee.

And that urge to protect, to comfort and provide had only grown as she had, building up within her and filling her with joy whenever she was able to help her family. Did it get her into trouble? Sure. She'd had a huge fight with her absolute cad of an uncle during her cousin Simon's graduation dinner, and that had definitely caused a rift, but all in all, she wouldn't change her protective drive for the world. So Cass could snap and get cranky all she wanted; Charity was going to do everything in her power to make sure her sister healed as quickly, safely and happily as she could.

Besides, it wasn't like she had any children of her own to worry about.

That thought had her mouth pressing into a thin line and she shoved it out of her head. She could worry about herself later. For the moment, the important thing was getting her sister up into bed so she could get settled. Cass didn't like how pain medicine made her feel and had been that way since she was a teen, but she'd had to take some for the long drive from the city hospital where she'd been taken care of and would definitely be needing a nap.

"Let me show you how to work it. It was made so you have complete control of your coming and going and don't have to ask us for anything."

"...Okay."

That restrained tone full of chagrin was gone from her sister's tone, leaving only a sort of weariness that made Charity's heart ache. Cass was the fiery and determined second oldest, the one who encouraged Charity when she was stuck on a problem and fearlessly following along on any of Charity's wild ideas. When she'd taken online certifications to learn how to repair their equipment and cars when she was seventeen, well Cass had happily followed along and got her certification too. Not because she loved mechanics, but because she liked hanging out and helping Charity.

And when Charity had needed help to get away from her ex, well Cass was right there too. In fact, she and he-who-would-not-be-talked-about almost came to blows. Of course, Charity had cut that off—it wasn't her baby sister's job to protect her—but it had finally helped cut the final straw.

"Hey, you okay?"

Charity blinked and realized that she'd paused when she'd bent over to open the clear cover over the buttons that operated the lift.

"Uh, yeah. I guess I just have a lot on my mind."

"You have been sleeping, right? I'm not clueless, you know. Drugged up, but not clueless. I know that ramp must have taken you a while."

"Eh, it wasn't that bad. Staining the wood took the longest, to be honest."

"Oh, it was stained? I'll have to take a better look at it."

"Mostly just some protective coats, but the wood was brighter than it looked when I ordered it online, and I know you're more of a dark oak than a birch girl, so I made it match your style."

Charity straightened to push her sister into the lift, but she paused when a cool hand gripped her warm one. "Thank you, Charity. Really. I... I'm gonna try to be better."

"Don't worry about it," she answered. And she meant it. "I'm just happy to have you home again. It's not the same without you."

"It wasn't the same without all of you either. Hospitals really aren't my thing."

Charity thought back to the many times their mother had been in those white, sterile halls before she passed. All the tears they'd shed as kids. How they'd had to say goodbye with the incessant beeping machines in the background.

"I don't blame you. But you're here now, but I'm going to take care of you, so don't you worry."

"And yourself too, right?"

"Sure," she answered as a matter of course. Even if she didn't quite know what that could possibly entail.

3

Alejandro

"Where is your lunch pail? I put it in the fridge for you last night, remember?"

"It's right here, Dad. Just like the last time you asked."

"Hey," Alejandro said, giving his daughter a tried and true dad-look. "Just because you've hit the double digits doesn't mean you can sass me."

Savannah just batted her lashes at him. It worked less since she had suddenly shot up, long and lanky just like her mother had been, but was still pretty effective at making Alejandro want to laugh or hug her until she called him embarrassing. "I'm basically eleven, actually."

"Oh, is that so?"

"Uh-huh."

"And who gave you permission to grow? If I recall right, I told you to stay a child forever."

"I guess I'm just rebellious that way."

"Well, you can rebellion your way right out to the bus stop. Do you have your backpack?"

It was her turn to give him a tried and true daughter-look right back at him. "*Yes*, Dad. Just like the other times you asked about that too. I think you're more nervous about me going to a new school than I am."

Alejandro grimaced, but his daughter wasn't wrong. She rarely was, actually. His little Savannah, who was already to his chest and trending to be over six feet tall, was too smart for her own good. Somehow, she'd gotten the best of both him and her mother, which was one of the reasons why school was so difficult for her.

But one of the reasons he'd agreed to take over the practice in such a small town was because their single school was actually quite accredited. And while Savannah had been pretty insistent on not ever being sent to a gifted school, they had a lot of programs and accelerated learning that would keep her occupied.

But more important than keeping her engaged and from being bored, it meant that there would be *other* students like her. There had to be—otherwise there wouldn't be a reason to have those programs. Savannah had been to three schools since the age of five, and while the first one had been great, the second one had her singled out and often picked on for her interests.

She'd kept it a secret, because of course she had, but when Alejandro had found out, he'd felt like a failure of a father. Especially since he found out because she'd headbutted a bully so hard that she'd chipped her top tooth with her bottom one. The fact that his daughter felt the need to hide that she was bullied to the point of misery from him to "protect him" was the last straw. So naturally, when his uncle-in-law had contacted him about taking over his practice after he retired, Alejandro had seen it as a chance for both of them to start over.

"It's a big deal, alright. Don't blame your dad for worrying."

Her face softened at that, and it was oh so easy to see so much of her mother written across her features. From her pale skin, which was considerably lighter than Alejandro's toffee'd tan, to the coppery auburn of her hair that was just beginning to darken as it did every fall and winter. Sometimes he wondered if there was any of him in her genes, but then her lips would quirk a certain way, or her eyes would get a gleam as she was reading a book, and there he was, bright and clear.

But then her hand reached up, resting on his cheek. "It'll be okay, Dad. It's just school."

Just school, hah. From anyone else it might have been a snarky, offhanded comment, but from Savannah, it was more than true. They *had* been through much worse.

"You're right, you're right. Let's head out."

The two of them exited their new house. Small compared to some of the doctors he knew, but perfect for them. Big enough that they could have their own space when they needed it, but small enough where none of it would feel empty. Aching. Full of echoes of who had been stolen from them and why.

No, their new house in the small town was just right, and he was actually looking forward to decorating it with his daughter as she came into her own tastes.

The bus trundled around the corner far too soon and Alejandro felt his palms begin to sweat. He liked to think that he maintained his cool, but Savannah still stood on tiptoe to kiss his cheek before bouncing off to the bus.

He stood there, watching as it drove off and until it went around the corner, and then it was time to start his day. Goodness knew he had a lot to do.

Going inside to grab his coffee thermos, he then headed to his car and started towards the practice he was going to take over.

He'd seen it in pictures before, and video walkthroughs with his uncle-in-law, but he hadn't seen it in person. Yet.

It wasn't a long drive, less than ten minutes, but it was nice. And it was nice to be out of the thick crowd and cloying traffic of San Diego too.

He hadn't been planning on the whole thing, about a year earlier. And if he was honest with himself, he wasn't really ready for it either. But when his uncle-in-law had called to broach the subject, mentioning that he wanted to retire but needed someone trustworthy to take over his practice as a small town's only doctor in the middle of New Mexico, Alejandro found *something* in him whispering that it might be exactly what he needed.

And then his uncle had outright *asked*, saying that he cared for the town and only wanted someone he could trust to replace him and treat them well, and *then* he'd been called to his daughter's school about the headbutting incident, and it was like the decision had been made for him.

There was a lot of work ahead of him though, and his stomach was twisting as he pulled up to the practice.

It was solid, quaint and all white with dark blue shutters and delicate awning. Much homier than the sterile conglomerate Alejandro had been working for previously.

Not that he had paid much attention to where he had

worked before. So often his days were all about going through the motions, blazing to life when it came to treating his patients but slipping into a sort of haze after that.

How many years had it been? Nearly a decade and yet, it was like there was a part of him that was missing. Often the only times he felt like a whole human was on his nights and days off at home with Savannah. His coworkers—because he didn't really have anything in the way of friends—told him he needed to have more of a work-life balance, that he needed to move on, but they didn't understand. Not really.

But his uncle's offer was forcing him to at least try to move on in a way, so he needed to hurry in and get situated before his first round of interviews. Because, along with his uncle-in-law retiring, his aunt-in-law had been the head receptionist and had retired as well, appointing her second-in-command as her replacement. The practice was so small it only needed two medical secretaries, but that left Alejandro to find the second half of his new team.

Maybe it had been overly ambitious to plan medical secretary interviews on his very first day in the office, but he wanted to get a new hire in and somewhat settled before the deluge of appointments came in.

The receptionist was already there, smiling as he came in. He'd met her over a video call, but never in person.

"Hello there," she said with a grin, extending her hand. She was a middle-aged woman with already graying hair that was braided into an impressive crown around her head. Portly and soft in a motherly way, she had a warmth to her that had Alejandro returning her grin without even having to think about it. "Pleasure to meet you face-to-face finally, Dr. Lumis."

"That it is," he answered with a nod. "Mrs. Whittaker, right?" She had the mildest of a southern twang, which surprised him. Not exactly the accent he expected in New Mexico. Then again, according to his uncle, people from all over the south tended to settle in different places on the rodeo circuit.

Huh... was the woman a retired trick rider? Or a rodeo clown? The thought had him more intrigued than he probably should have been. But it wasn't exactly like he knew a lot of cowboys or rodeo stars in San Diego, which was where he'd been born and raised.

"I was the last time I checked. Now, we've got the first interview coming in about an hour, so how about I walk you to your office and show you our systems?"

Alejandro nodded, flashing her what he hoped was a winning grin. The computer systems they used to keep track of patient charts and scheduling was usually his least favorite part of any job, if only because there didn't seem to be a national sort of standard. And even though he'd only changed where he was employed twice before taking over the practice, learning a whole new system irritated him to no end.

Oh well. He could take a little irritation compared to all the good. The fresh start. It was the blank slate that he and Savannah needed to start over.

He just hoped that they really would be able to find happiness in the small town.

4

—————

Charity

"Help me! Charity! Help me, please!!!"

Charity's head whipped back and forth, trying to find the source of the voice.

"Cass!" she called out, peering through the black, trying to pump her feet, but she just wasn't moving. Why wasn't she moving!? "Cass! Where are you!?"

"Help me! You're supposed to help me!"

"I'm trying!"

Panic rose in Charity's chest, making the back of her tongue taste acrid and bitter. She pushed her body harder, feeling nauseous, but she couldn't move. In fact, the ground below her wasn't even ground. It was thick, ashen glop that was pulling her down, down, down, like quicksand.

"Cass!"

And then the darkness was over her head, dragging her away from her sister's screams.

Charity jolted awake, chest heaving and breath harsh through her nose. Adrenaline was pumping through her so hard that she was nauseous, and it took her a couple of minutes to realize where she was.

It was the familiar fabric of the recliner chair underneath her fingers that grounded her first, then the familiar smell of the vanilla cleaner that Papa loved to use in the kitchen. That was enough, and she was able to heave a few breaths to steady herself. It had been a week or so since her last bad nightmare, but that definitely wasn't long enough.

"I thought I heard you up."

Charity's gaze flitted to the open entryway that led to the kitchen, seeing Papa entering with two cups of coffee. He handed her the larger one, doctored up with plenty of cream but no sugar before sitting across from her.

"I wasn't screaming again, was I?"

He shook his head, expression caring in a way that made her feel so warm and loved. If she could bottle that feeling, she would hand it out to everyone she knew who didn't have a parent who was kind and trustworthy.

"No. But it just felt like maybe you were having a bad night."

"I was."

"I've said this before, but you know it's not your fault, right?"

Charity swallowed her coffee, hot and comforting down her throat, but didn't answer. Sure, they had talked about it. And maybe intellectually she knew, but that didn't abate her guilt at all. Guilt and worry. Maybe if it was level-headed

Clara, she wouldn't have to worry so much, but Cass was an awful patient and always pushed herself too hard.

"It's my job to protect the family," she said finally when her father's gaze grew too sweet, too kind. "I'm the eldest."

"You are, you definitely are. But that doesn't mean you can do everything for everyone without giving yourself some slack."

"I don't need slack," she said with a wan grin. "Slack makes my skin itch and my mind wander."

He looked like he wanted to say something else, his eyes with a look only a father could give, but instead he just quietly drank his coffee with her.

Charity always liked that about Papa. He put his foot down when he needed to, but mostly he let them all go their own way and do their own thing. The three youngest had left and tried college at some point, but Charlie had come back after his first year, saying it wasn't for him, and Clara only bothered to get her associate's degree.

Only Cici, the youngest of their brood, had decided to go the whole way and was finishing up her bachelor's. She'd wanted to come back when the whole car accident had happened, but Cass had insisted that she stay and finish her classes; they could hang out as much as she wanted during the summer break.

The thought that Cass would probably still be in her wheelchair by then made her stomach flip. Cass was so *independent* and had shared most of the chore duty on their ranch with Charity. And although she was sure her other siblings would step up, she was also sure that it would hurt Cass that she couldn't help.

"Thanks for the coffee," Charity said, draining the rest and standing. "I better get ready. Today Cass and I are supposed to see that new doctor of hers."

"Ah, yes. That will be much more convenient than hauling her to the city every week." Charity opened her mouth, but he just waved a hand. "I know you would be happy to, but that's beside the point. I'm glad we were able to work out a program where she has a doctor to monitor her here and do her check-ups, so we only have to go to the city once a month."

Charity nodded. He was right, of course. It wouldn't have been possible just a month earlier with their previous town doctor, a nice older man who knew almost everyone from birth. Although he was a great doctor, he wasn't a physical therapist. But apparently his replacement had started as a physical therapist before changing his career course. Curious, but Charity had been pretty relieved when the Doc had called Papa and told him the situation in the hopes that it might help Cass.

"Right. So, I'm going to go get ready."

Taking her mug to the kitchen, she went about readying herself before heading to Cass's room. One knock, two knocks, then a shout asking if she died, and Cass finally flung the door open.

"You're wearing that?" Charity asked, eyebrows raising.

Now she was the last one to really care about fashion—she liked pretty clothes, but most of the time they just weren't on her radar—but her sister was wearing stained sweats and an oversized hoody that pooled around her hips in her chair.

"Why? Wasn't aware I needed to doll myself up for the guy who was going to poke and prod me."

"You don't, but that doesn't mean you want to look like a garbage pile either."

"Garbage pile?"

"I can see the tomato soup you ate yesterday on your pants and the cranberry juice from your breakfast."

"...fine. Give me fifteen minutes and I'll change."

"Right. Want me to pack anything for you?"

"A will to live?"

It was a joke, but wow did it bite at Charity's apprehension. Her fingers itched, and once more she felt like she was shoved into a skin that was too tight, her heart beating so hard that it would erupt from her shell. Once the whole doctor appointment was done, she needed a long ride on her horse and maybe a couple of hours underneath one of their tractors.

Unlike the other extended-family Millers, they didn't have any sort of industry or business with their small ranch. They tried their best to be self-sufficient and maintain their wealth, but by and large, none of them were interested in all the drama that seemed to come from trying to maintain billion-dollar corporations.

Not that they were poor. Hardly. Charity couldn't really wrap her mind around how much money they had from generation after generation of family wealth and all the investments that were in Papa's name. But no one in their branch was going to be a billionaire, and Charity was just fine with that.

"Fresh out of those. I'll see if I can pick one up in town."

"That'd be great. You can clear out. I don't need you to dress me."

Charity wanted to argue, her steps hesitating as the urge to insist otherwise bubbled up. But she shoved that down and gave her sister a nod, heading back out to try to occupy herself for fifteen minutes. Sure, she was a worrywart and she wanted to make sure Cass didn't accidentally hurt herself, but insinuating that her sister was too much of an invalid to even dress herself would only make her livid. And when Cass was livid, she did brash things. It was a weakness they all had.

Fifteen minutes was just short enough not to do anything actually involved but just too long to lollygag around, but Cass kept to her word and rolled herself out of her room. Charity stood to the side, letting her sister direct herself. She made it about halfway down the hall before stopping, her arms shaking as they tried to force the wheels of her chair further.

It hurt Charity to watch her struggle. She wanted to wipe the sweat from Cass's brow and rub her hands until they didn't ache anymore. She wanted to find the softest yet toughest gloves for her protection and make sure Cass didn't have to hurt any more than she had to.

But she also knew that any attempt to baby her younger sister would have the woman snapping at her, teeth bared and temper sparking. So, she waited. And waited. Waited for what seemed to be an eternity before Cass finally sighed.

"I think I gotta tap out now."

"Okay," Charity said simply, coming up behind her sister to grip the handles of her wheelchair and push it forward.

It didn't take them overly long to get her in the car, but Charity didn't like the hisses of pain. Maybe she needed to invest in a van and a wheelchair lift? That seemed like it would be better for driving Cass around. But she'd have to float the idea by her sister first, knowing that she could take it badly.

Maybe anyone else would have been exhausted trying to navigate around Cass's prickliness about her injury, but Charity understood it. She got the frustration; she got the fear. She even got how her sister hated being helpless. Sure, it wasn't pleasant, but neither was being almost killed in a car accident.

"You're thinking too hard," Cass remarked, her head tipped back against the headrest. "I can feel it from here."

"Well, I might have a lot to think about."

"Sounds fake."

That startled a laugh from Charity and the bubbling of mirth had her eyes widening. When was the last time she'd laughed with her sister? Had it been the night of the car accident? It seemed so, and that was depressing enough to sober her mirth.

"You caught me. I'm just a simple cowgirl full of simple thoughts."

Cass huffed in what maybe could have been a laugh, but at least she half-smiled and that was a victory in and of itself.

They didn't talk much other than that on the ride to town, but the mood wasn't awful. More... wary. Maybe a little weary. But it wasn't the same pinched, barely contained fear that had been biting at Charity's legs ever since the night of the crash.

Getting Cass out of the car wasn't exactly easy either, and every suppressed grunt or groan from her sister had Charity's stomach twisting up tightly. She knew better than to say anything about it, however, and just pressed her lips into a thin line as she walked into the quaint building that she was somewhat familiar with.

Charity had never been much for doctors and had been lucky to always pretty much be in excellent health. She'd had a misstep once as a kid and broke her arm when she fell from the barn loft, but other than that it had been pretty much smooth sailing. Cass had the record for zero broken bones in the family, actually. Or at least she had before a drunk driver crashed into her and shattered far too much of her skeleton.

There was her stomach, flipping again as she remembered the surgeon telling them all the pins they had to put in. And screws. And other things that didn't sound like they belonged in a person. It was as terrifying as it was impressive, and she didn't think Cass even understood how absolutely incredible she was.

But that was alright. Charity would be around plenty to remind her.

"Oh, hey there, lovelies! I haven't seen you in ages. How are we today?"

Charity blinked and looked up at the receptionist, vaguely recognizing her. "We're doing good, thank you. How have you been?"

"Oh, you know. Keeping busy. Goodness, your hair has gotten so long!"

Charity blinked at the woman as she came around the desk and gave her a hug. Thankfully she had the good sense not to try that with Cass. "It has?" She supposed that she hadn't cut her long, auburn hair in... was it three years now? Maybe four? Mostly she just kept it in one long braid, so it was out of her way. "Huh, I guess I didn't notice."

"Huh, show off!" the woman said good-naturedly, her grin soft and warm. Something pinged in the back of Charity's mind, and she wondered just how old the woman was and if she was single. If she was... well, it wouldn't hurt to introduce her to Papa, would it?

"Mrs. Whittaker, there seems to be a mix-up—"

All the heads turned to the deep, slightly accented voice coming from one of the few doorways in the room. Charity wasn't sure what she was expecting, but it certainly wasn't a man who checked off tall, dark, handsome, *and* well dressed all in one fell swoop.

His shoulders were broad, taking up most of the doorway he was standing in, and his thick brows were drawn together in a concerned expression before he noticed there were others in the room and startled. His skin was a beautiful sort of candied ocher, rich and deep like he'd just walked off a vibrantly sunny beach and not a small-town doctor's office. His hair was thick and black, with the slightest bit of salt and pepper just beginning to grace his temples.

Wow. Oh wow. Charity felt her mouth dry up and her mind quickly scribbled down a dozen and one positive attributes about the man. It was almost embarrassing, and not for the first time, she was glad that no one could read her mind.

"Wait, is it two o'clock already?" He bent his arm so that the navy button-up he was wearing revealed a fairly subdued watch, and then those thick brows of his were drawing together again. *Goodness,* he had bone structure that wasn't fair. High and wide cheekbones with a defined edge, and a classic jaw with a cleft in his chin.

He was like a movie star or former model and—oh *shoot,* she was staring, wasn't she?

"Apologies, Miss..." He looked down at the tablet in his hand and scrolled a moment before seeming to recover. "Miss Miller. I'm still settling in. I'll be ready in a couple of minutes, if you don't mind."

"Sure. Do what you gotta do."

The man gave a grateful nod then disappeared back into the room he came from, leaving the three women staring at the empty doorway.

"Certainly different from our last doctor, isn't he?" Mrs. Whittaker asked, chuckling lightly.

Charity could only nod, her attention still lingering on the door.

Maybe if she wasn't so bone-tired and wrapped up in her sister's healing, she would have had the wherewithal to be embarrassed. But when was the last time she had even looked at a man? Sure, her divorce was finalized a while ago, but the whole messy affair had entirely turned her off from dating. She hadn't had a flicker of interest since then.

Not that she was *interested* in the doctor. That would be ridiculous. But she couldn't deny that maybe—definitely—there was an attraction there, warm and inviting and fizzing along the top of her mind like a soda.

"Hey, where's the bathroom around here?" Cass asked, rolling herself out of Charity's grip. The receptionist told her, and Cass trundled herself off, glaring at her older sister as if she was daring her to say something.

Charity almost did, but she caught herself and let her sister roll off to do her thing. "Will you just leave the door unlocked?"

"Only if you guard it. Wouldn't want someone to come in and startle me off the toilet."

It was a funny image, but Charity managed not to snort. "Yeah, I can do that."

She let her sister enter the bathroom then moved to stand in front of the door. Unfortunately, that had the side effect of leaving Charity alone with her thoughts, and they went right back to the doctor.

When had she gotten so "thirsty," she believed it was called? He clearly wasn't from around the town and was probably some hoity-toity city slicker who thought with his wallet and didn't even know how to change a tire. Or sharpen a tractor blade. Or how to amend the soil of a garden.

Extra unfortunately, Cass was still in the bathroom when the doctor returned, looking more composed and expecting a patient. It was only then that her mind kicked in that she didn't even *like* doctors. With the exception of the nice old man who used to own the practice. Even before anything happened with her mother.

Nope, that particular bias started back when she first began to hit puberty and her pediatrician told her that her migraines were just part of being a woman. And then after that, that it was normal for her period to feel like a horse kicked her right in the gut. It took *years*, and a whole lot of money that most people didn't have access to, to find out that she had a hormonal imbalance that was affecting her whole reproductive system.

Maybe if the doctor had *listened* to her, everything could have been caught earlier and she would have been saved a lot of pain.

But *no*, it had taken her studying and researching her—

Actually, she didn't even want to think about any of that, walling it off in the back of her mind where it was supposed to stay.

Thankfully the door opened behind her and Cass rolled out. "Oh, hey, Doc. I think you're waiting for me?"

"That I am. After you, Miss Miller."

Cass nodded, going where the doctor gestured, and Charity automatically fell into line behind her sister. But that stopped quickly when Cass stopped moving and craned her neck over her shoulder.

"Can I help you?"

Charity blinked at her. "Uh, I was just gonna, uh—"

"I can handle my doctor's appointment on my own. You can wait outside—or, even better—go occupy yourself doing something *actually fun*."

"I don't need—"

"Blah, blah, blah, I'm not listening. Guess you'll have to go and do something you enjoy doing."

"… you and Papa teamed up for this, didn't you?"

"I have no idea what you're talking about. Byeeee."

If the doctor had anything to say, it didn't come out of his mouth. Instead he was just smiling slightly, seemingly amused. Great. She was happy that they could entertain the guy from the city who probably had all sorts of misconceptions about southerners and western folk.

"You're welcome to stay however long you like," he said politely. "I'm sure Mrs. Whittaker would love the company."

"No, kick her out," Cass said, fulling rolling out of sight. "Make her go socialize or at least not work for an hour or so."

The doctor didn't do that. Instead he just smiled, tipped his head, and headed after Cass. Charity heard a door close and found herself alone, the only sound in the room being Mrs. Whittaker's surprisingly hard typing. Charity turned to her, prepared to at least try a conversation, but then the phone rang, and the woman was picking it right up.

Okay, so no conversation there.

Charity stood there a minute, trying to decide what to do, before shrugging and heading out onto the street. She hadn't really been in town much since the accident, and it was kind of nice to be back. Idly, she wondered if her high score was still sitting on the most popular pinball machine at the local bar.

Well, maybe it was a good time to go check.

If felt mildly wrong to just walk away from her sister, especially since the last few months of her life had completely revolved around her sibling, but the idea of sitting in the reception area, quiet and alone in her thoughts, was completely unappealing.

It didn't take her long to walk to the bar, but it didn't take long to walk anywhere in the small town. It would take less than an hour to walk from one end to the other, by her estimation, but she liked it just fine.

But then she actually reached the bar. She'd barely walked into the front door before everything about Cass's accident rushed back to her.

The horrible sounds over the phone. The way Cass didn't answer her, even as she called her name. The fact that it was a drunk driver that had collided with her flashed through her mind. That it had just been a single human, inebriated and disoriented by the storm, that had almost taken her sister away.

It was so much, so intense, that before she even could parse out her thoughts, she was turning on her heel and striding right back out of the bar.

By the time she really came back to herself, she was at her truck, staring at her faint reflection in the vehicle's windows like it would tell her something.

It didn't, of course. But it probably would have been much more alarming if it had.

With a sigh, she clambered into her truck and left the doctor's office, going to a specific spot that she remembered from back when she was in high school and had just gotten her license.

Just like the bar, it didn't take long to get there, and soon she was parked in a tiny little lot in the center of the town's park. That wasn't very huge either, but it was the town's pride and joy, and the parking lot was surrounded by weeping willows, blue Chinese wisteria, and pink mimosa trees. They provided plenty of shade to keep things cool and were much more beautiful than they had any right to be. It was a parking lot, after all.

But to Charity, it was more of her favorite nap spot, so she clambered into the back of her truck, grabbed a thick comforter from her travel-trunk that was permanently strapped in, then spread it out to lay down on.

It was... nice. Just lying there, looking up at the afternoon sky tucked behind the blue, pink, and green of the foliage. She could feel a breeze across her body, and it soothed her in an unfamiliar sort of way, one that reminded her of simpler times.

But had her life ever really been simple? Her mother had passed so young, so suddenly, and even though Papa tried his best, Charity suddenly had to grow up so fast. But what kid didn't when a parent passed too soon?

And maybe she grew up too fast, because then she was falling into *his* arms so easily. She had thought he was the love of her life, let herself get swept up in it. She was just so *young*, and by the time she was nineteen...

Her thoughts trailed off, not wanting to ruin such a peaceful place with the storms of her past. There were people out there who had it so much worse, and she was crying over five-year-old heartbreak.

Well, it was more than five years, but that was beside the point. And that point was that she needed to stop letting ghosts haunt her and live her life. She had thought she was doing so well until Cass's accident, and suddenly she found herself pushed into the same spot she'd been in when she was just a kid.

Worried that someone she loved was going to die.

Thankfully Cass was well away from that danger, knock on wood, but she'd been close that night and the fear still hadn't faded. At least not for Charity. Maybe in a year or two, sure. But at the moment, she couldn't even walk into a bar.

Time slipped away in that hazy place somewhere between

a nap and just relaxing. Before she knew it, her phone was beeping with the alarm she'd set when she'd left the doctor's office and it was time for her to head back.

She felt less in her head as she drove, watching the town as it passed her by. Perhaps that was the only reason why she spotted the young girl standing on the corner, looking up and down at her phone then around herself in the universal sign for being absolutely lost.

Huh, that was unusual. There wasn't really enough of a town to get lost in, but Charity couldn't shake the feeling. And when she looked at the absolutely massive basket at her feet that was teeming with cellophane-wrapped items, she figured she might as well see if the young girl needed help.

Pulling over, she stayed a reasonable distance away then called out. "Hey, you need some directions?"

The girl started, her big eyes wide. Goodness, she couldn't have been older than thirteen, all long limbs but still with a tiny bit of baby fat. It wasn't unusual for young kids to walk home from school alone, but she wasn't heading towards either of the housing areas. Instead, she was facing the boulevard, which would bring her to the business center of the town.

"Uh, yeah, actually. I'm going to the doctor's office, but I think I got turned around."

Huh, life sure had a funny way of working out. "The doctor's office? I'm actually headed there myself."

"Oh, that works! You can just give me a ride."

At that, Charity had to tip her head back and laugh. That only lasted a moment, however, before she realized that the girl was serious.

"Haven't your parents told you not to accept rides from strangers? That's dangerous."

"Normally, yeah," the girl said as cool as a cucumber.

What was it with kids these days? When Charity was young, she always got flustered around adults who were so much bigger and seemed to know what to do.

Of course, that had changed after her mother had died... huh.

"But this is a small town, so it's not like we're in a giant city. Plus, I've already memorized your license plate and texted it to myself. If I were to go missing, they'd just look up my phone history and see you right there." As if to prove it, she recited it like it was nothing, her gaze never leaving Charity's.

Maybe she shouldn't have been amused, but she was. The girl reminded her of when her sister Cass had been young, so sure and determined of every little thing. "Well don't you have life figured out?"

"Hardly. But I'm alright at reading people and I can tell you're safe. Mostly. For a ride, at least."

"Anyone ever tell you that you don't really talk like a kid?"

"Incessantly. But anyway, let's go."

Charity laughed again at the random girl telling her what to do, but also figured why not? The girl was right that Charity was safe and wouldn't hurt her, but the next person might not be if she chose to leave the young teen on the corner, looking vulnerable.

Not that she thought that anyone in their small town would actually hurt her, but still, it never hurt to be careful.

"Here, let me put that into the back for you," Charity said as the girl lugged over the truly giant basket. She wedged it in next to the travel-trunk so it wouldn't fall anywhere, then went back around to her driver's side. The girl slid into the passenger's seat like there was nothing strange about getting into an unknown woman's truck and settled back.

It was strange, it was funny, but most of all it was surprising enough to keep Charity out of her head, so she just shook it and started driving towards the doctor's office. As she went, she couldn't help but hope the basket was some sort of welcoming gift to the new town doctor and the young girl wasn't sick herself.

There was far too much hurt going around for that.

5

———————

Alejandro

"Alright, do you have any other questions or concerns?"

"Not at the moment. I think you answered just about all of them. Hope I didn't run up your schedule too much."

Alejandro shook his head. "Not at all. I knew this appointment would go long because we needed to get a baseline, map out our goals, and discuss all the information that a medical file can't tell us."

"Funny, the doctors in the hospital treat those like the Bible. Didn't think you'd be much different."

He smiled down at his new patient—Cass she wanted him to call her—who was sweating slightly as she slid down from the exam table into her wheelchair. Her light brown hair was mussed around her head, but that didn't take away from her striking features. There was something unusual about her face, with wide, sharp cheekbones, catlike eyes and a square jaw that was much stronger than many women. The woman who had come in with her had shared those same features, enough to let him know they were probably related. Twins maybe? They looked to be around the same age.

"The chart is important, don't get me wrong," he answered with a grin, "but it's not the end-all, be-all. Your chart may tell me that you are allergic to bees, but you will tell me that it's only a mild allergy unless you're stung near your neck. It could say you broke your arm when you were a kid, but you are the only one who can tell me how it aches when the pressure changes or how a muscle catches when you move just so. We're a team, you and I, so we have to work together to hit the goals we've just set."

Cass grinned, her teeth starkly white against her peachy, tanned skin. "You know, I think that would have sounded pretty cheesy from anybody else. But it was almost passable from you."

He huffed a laugh at that and felt relieved that he and the woman seemed to be getting on. Sure, he didn't have to be friends with every patient, but Cassidy Miller was going to be an intense case that he spent a lot of time with. He wanted them to get along.

It helped that he was impressed by her strength, both physical and of character. But he also felt terrible for her. Her accident was severe, and she was very lucky to be alive. He'd seen the results of similar wrecks on far too many cadavers in medical school.

Actually, for being such a small town, he was going to be flexing quite a lot of his medical training. He had another patient coming in later in the week also for intense follow-up care after being struck by lightning in the same storm that Miss Miller had had her accident in.

Yeah, actually struck by lightning and survived. Incredible. He and his coworkers would have been fighting like cats and dogs to get a chance to lay their hands on a case like that back in San Diego.

"Hey, this all has me exhausted, so would you mind wheeling me out? Feels like my hands might fall off."

"That's going to be pretty common after our first few sessions," Alejandro said with a nod. "And I have no problem with that. Let's go see if your companion ended up waiting around."

"My sister? Gosh, I hope not. Fingers crossed she actually took the time to do something for herself."

Ah, sister. So not a twin, she probably would have said that if she was. "Something she has difficulty doing?"

"You have no idea."

He gripped the handles of her wheelchair and pushed her out. Cass seemed to perk up when the reception area was empty, only Mrs. Whittaker who was on the phone. "Looks like she made it out."

"Wow, she actually left." Cass leaned her head back to smile at him. "Wanna wheel me out to that nice porch of yours? I feel like I haven't just sat in the sun in ages."

"Well, it's a shaded porch, but I'm happy to do that."

He continued on, but as soon as he was near the door, he could hear a familiar voice just on the other side.

Confused, he hit the handicapped button to open the door and was surprised to see both his daughter Savannah and the stubborn sister from earlier sitting on the floor of the porch, playing cards.

That was just about the last thing he expected.

"Stuck," Savannah said, her hand pausing to rest over one of the piles of cards. But the sister kept on playing card after card in an impossible blur. "Aw, come on, are you really gonna beat a kid?"

"You've won seven times already. Don't think you can play the kid card now."

"Apparently I can't play any cards, *furiendo*."

"*Furiendo*?" Finally the sister stopped and her hand went to a pile opposite of Savannah's hand. "Stuck."

"About time. Three, two, *one!*"

Both of them drew a card at the same time and set it down on the center mess, and then hands were flying again, too fast to see. They both wore intense looks of concentration, and it would have been quite amusing if he wasn't so confused as to why his daughter was playing cards with a stranger when she should have been in school or at home.

"The first time off on your own in months and you've already found a new Speed acolyte," Cass said.

"A what?" Alejandro asked sharply.

"It's a card game Charity likes," she answered matter-of-factly.

Charity, huh? That was certainly a name. Funny that two sisters would share a name with the same starting consonant.

Cass continued, "She tries to get everyone to play it with her, but she always wins."

"Until today," Savannah retorted, and Alejandro recognized that tone from her. It was the one that meant she was thoroughly caught up in something, her gifted mind fully occupied in a way it rarely was.

"I wish I could say she's wrong," Charity said as her hands continued to fly. "But she's beaten me more than anyone else ever has. I—"

"Done!" Savannah cried, slapping her hand down.

"No fair," Charity said with a wide, easy grin that caught Alejandro's attention more than it should have. She had the same interesting face structure as Cass, but more angular, with a squarishness to her nose that balanced everything else. There was also a sharpness to her eyes, making them look even more catlike than her sister.

It shouldn't have worked, all of it was too much, too intense, but there was something about her, wearing that blinding smile, that made her look otherworldly in the best way.

"I was distracted by your dear old dad."

"That sounds like a 'you' problem and not a 'me' problem."

"You really don't talk like a kid, you know."

"Yeah, you said that earlier."

"Just felt like I should reiterate it."

Normally. When anyone said something like that about his daughter, Alejandro would sweep in and read them the riot act. His daughter was brilliantly gifted and sweet as could be, especially after everything she'd lived through. But something about the way the woman said it seemed like a compliment, and Savannah definitely appeared to take it as such.

As if to prove the point, Savannah sat back and shot the woman her own grin. "You don't talk like an adult, you know."

"I don't?"

Cass laughed, rolling her wheelchair forward on her own. "It's not your words, Charity. It's your tone. You don't condescend just because people are young."

"No, I just condescend when people are mean."

Then they both were laughing, and Savannah finally stood

to give him a hug. It reminded him of the fact that she shouldn't be there at all.

"Hey, what's going on? Why aren't you at school?" he said.

"I texted you, but I couldn't really get a signal at the school. Their day ends weirdly early here. Two-thirty instead of three. You'd think they'd have mentioned that at least once."

"They didn't... did they?" Alejandro tried to sort through his memory, but so much of the past few months were a blur. "I don't think they did."

"Me either. But anyway, I decided I'd walk here to say hi. They gave me a whole basket to give to you and I didn't want to haul it on the bus."

"No, so you just manually hauled it here."

"Not all the way, this lady gave me a ride."

That made Alejandro's eyebrows move up to his hairline. "You what now?"

"*Daaad*," she said, no doubt sensing what was coming.

"That's not exactly safe, *miha*."

"I told her as much," Charity said, standing and offering her hand to shake. "But we watch out for each other here in this small town, so if she was gonna do it, this is the place to risk it."

Alejandro didn't know quite how to act, but he shook Charity's hand. He was upset that his daughter just hopped into the car of a stranger, but he was also happy to see her at his practice. She'd been riding the bus home on her own most days, so he'd had no idea the school day ended early. "Well, thank you for bringing her right here."

"Of course. It worked out well, considering Cass was already here." The woman's gaze returned to her sister. "We good to go?"

"Oh yeah, we're good to go. As soon as we get home, I am taking a monster of a nap."

And then Charity's beaming grin was pointing right at him again. "You worked my sister over that much, huh?"

"Something like that," he answered, trying to sound friendly but professional. He wasn't sure if he nailed it, something about the woman's beaming grin grabbing far too much of his brain. Goodness, the Miller sisters were unfairly attractive folks, weren't they? "See you next week?" That was directed to his patient, of course.

"Wouldn't miss it."

The two of them headed off, going around to the small side lot, and Alejandro turned his attention back to his daughter and the ridiculously oversized basket in the corner of the porch. "That doesn't even look real, you know."

"Right? Can you carry it in for me? My hands hurt."

"I wonder why..." he mused teasingly, grabbing the basket and heading inside. But as it set it on the reception desk, allowing Mrs. Whittaker to coo over it, he couldn't help but look out the window and watch the two sisters drive away. If all of his patients were as interesting and amiable as those two... well, it was easier than ever to believe that the new practice would really be his second chance.

6

Charity

More mail from her ex. Ugh. Not the best way to start the day. Thankfully, it was easy enough to bury it in ranch chores, checking up on the livestock, feeding the chickens, and maintaining their equipment.

And she needed to bury herself, because otherwise she would float around Cass, mother-henning her until she drove her sister absolutely insane. It wasn't like Charity could help it. She just wanted to make sure her sister was safe, protected, and able to heal. But her sister wouldn't be able to heal if she was half-insane with irritation, so chores it was.

Besides, it wasn't like she had anything else going for her. No husband. No children. No interest in dating. Her whole life was the ranch and her family. So, she committed to her grind, until it was time to take Cass to the doctor again. Who knew a week could have gone so fast? But taking her little sister to the doctor made her feel more in control and less like a wildly spinning weathervane.

That was probably why cold fear shot through her when she came out of the bathroom and saw Charlie with the keys to his jeep.

"What'cha doin'?" she asked, something uncertain blooming in her stomach.

"There you are. I thought you were sleeping in, so I was just going to take Cass to the doc. Figured I should meet him; sounds like a cool guy."

"No, that's alright," Charity said quickly. "I got it."

"It's no problem, really. Clara said she'd handle my chores too, so why don't you take a bre—"

"Thank you, but I got it. I do. I really do."

His eyebrows furrowed in that way they always did when he thought she was being particularly insane. "You're aware you're not our mom, right? You don't have to."

She knew her little brother and knew he was trying to say it in jest, but it didn't quite land with her, making her stomach curdle. "Just let me do it, okay?"

His face twisted in contrition, color rising on his cheeks. "Yeah, of course. I'm sorry, sis. You know I didn't mean it."

"I know, don't worry about it." She moved down the hall and stood on tiptoe to kiss him on the cheek. It wasn't fair that he was so tall. Didn't he know *she* was the eldest? The disrespect, honestly. "Thank you for understanding."

"Of course. If we don't have each other's backs, what do we have?"

"Nothing at all," she answered, repeating her family's common mantra. Sure, maybe they weren't the richest of the Millers, but they didn't have any prodigal sons or tyrannical fathers obsessed with money.

Granted, Bradley had apparently come back into the fold and her Uncle McLintoc had retired, but she wasn't sure if she could trust that second one.

"You want to get Cass for me while I load up some drinks and snacks? I'll probably have some waiting to do during her appointment."

"I think I can manage that."

Charlie headed off, and Charity went about what she needed to do until the two met her in front of the house. Charlie was a good kid. Standing tall and broad with sandy brown hair, he could pass for one of her strapping cousins in Montana. Although he'd dropped out of college, he was the dedicated sort. If she asked something of him, he did it, even though it was clear that he was always looking for something... *more.*

She didn't know what, of course. She could hardly figure out what her own restlessness wanted half the time. But she knew that he seemed just as uninterested in dating as she was, turning down anyone who was interested and insisting he just didn't have the capacity for any sort of relationship.

"You ready to take me to my torture session?" Cass asked once she was safely inside the truck.

"Aw, come on, they can't be that bad."

"Last time he just looked at how well I could raise my arms, wiggle my toes, and my grip strength, but I was still sweating."

"You were there for an hour and a half. There's no way that's all you did."

"Well, there was a lot of talking too, and resisting when he pushed down on my arms or elbows or something, but that's pretty much it. Today he's walking me through the PT room, so I'm sure that's gonna hurt *real* bad."

Despite her words, there was a broad grin across her face, and Charity was glad. It was like her sister was coming back in slices, and it made her incredibly happy to see it. She'd been worried for a bit there...

"Oh, by the way, this is going to be a longer session, probably two hours, so take your time on whatever it is you want to do."

"Two hours? Isn't that overly long?" Charity got the point of PT, but her sister could barely roll herself around for five minutes straight; how was she supposed to work for almost twenty times that?

"Like I said, most of it is a walkthrough, explaining what I need to do, why and how to do certain things."

"Uh-huh."

"Just trust the Doc, okay? He actually listens and seems to know what he's talking about."

"If you say so."

"And he's not exactly hard on the eyes either."

"If you say so," Charity repeated, trying to go for careless but missing it by a mile. Shoot.

"Don't pretend like you didn't notice. Guy is a dreamboat. I'm trying to figure out if he's married or not since he has a kid but no wedding ring."

Charity swallowed, her stomach curdling again. It had been doing that a lot lately. Weird. "Aiming for a doctor now? I can't say I disapprove."

She let out a snort that was certainly loud. "Not for me, *silly*. I've got enough on my plate right now. I mean for *you*."

Charity clenched the steering wheel much harder than she needed to. "Don't, Cass."

"What? Come on, isn't it time to get out there? And the two of you certainly seemed—"

"*Don't*, Cass."

"...alright. Fine. You can let me out in the front."

Cass was stubborn, that was for sure, but at least she seemed to know when to lay off. Charity was grateful for that, and as repayment, she didn't try to argue about following her sister as she dropped her off.

...barely.

But once Cass was safely inside the office, Charity drove to the bar again, figuring that the previous time was just a fluke from too much stress and worry all at once.

She felt like she arrived quicker than a blink and didn't even have time to get anxious before she was inside. The Stumblin' Bin wasn't exactly the most high-brow place in the state, but it wasn't dirty or skeezy and Charity was fine with that. This time, she was able to walk right up to the bar without that same panic setting in on her, but she hesitated when the bartender asked her what she wanted.

She didn't have any problems with drinking, she didn't. And she didn't think that alcohol was bad either. But now there was this new connection in her brain that associated alcohol with a terrible, horrifying night of her life. She wasn't sure if it was something she could unlearn, but the sour smell of beer was quickly making her nauseous.

"Quarters," she said quickly, sliding a five-dollar bill across the bar.

"Aren't you a little old for arcade machines?" someone beside her slurred, sending more wafts of stale alcohol into her personal space.

She didn't understand why so many of them liked the pale, uninteresting taste of what was basically wheat soda. She liked whiskey and bourbon when she wanted to be rowdy and wine when she wanted to relax. Or... she used to. All of that was pretty up in the air at the moment.

"Aren't you a little bit drunk to be handing out any sort of life advice to people?" Charity retorted without looking. She didn't need to look. She knew exactly who it was, Butch Taylor and his garbage bag of opinions that always flowed from his garbage bag face, which fit his garbage bag of a personality.

"Funny, coming from some rich girl living off her family's legacy."

Charity rolled her eyes. She was familiar with the people who resented her and her family. She was aware that, out of sheer luck, she had a lot of advantages other people didn't, and her life would have been a lot more stressful if her ancestors hadn't made it so nice and cushy for her. She was aware she'd never have to worry about bills, or being broke, and that was the daily reality for others.

But Papa had always insisted on all of them developing skills so that they could provide for themselves if suddenly the money mystically dried up. Charity knew how to be a lead ranch hand, she was borderline a heavy equipment mechanic, able to do basic repairs and maintenance. She knew how to cook, how to hunt, and how to grow food. Yes, she would always agree that she was lucky, blessed even, but she would never, ever be just a rich girl.

"Does that excuse make you feel better about the utter sad sack you've ended up?"

The bartender handed her a cup of quarters, his eyes flicking between her and Butch.

"What did you say?"

Charity fixed him with her sweetest smile. "Let's not pretend you don't know what I mean. You undercut the accomplishments and actions of everyone around you.

Because if you admitted that all those people are going places, you'd have to realize that you're going nowhere but this stool in this bar, and it's nobody's fault but your own."

He laughed, bitter and cloying, and suddenly Charity wasn't interested in the pinball machine anymore. Not with him staring daggers at her back the whole time.

"You really got me figured out, don't you? Easy to do from that high hill you're on, huh?"

"Only because you make yourself such an easy target." Setting the cup of quarters down, she shoved it back towards the bartender. "You know what, I changed my mind. Think I need some better company."

She realized it was a bad decision to come to the bar, pinball machine or not, and headed out. But she wasn't far enough before she heard Butch mutter under his breath.

"Piece of work, huh? No wonder her ex left."

The words bit into her soul, their teeth sinking into the softest parts of her, the parts that she liked to deny existed at all. She whirled on her heel, temper flaring, and it would have been so easy to stride forward and start the fight that was sparking along her fingertips and curling her fists.

...but no.

She didn't.

She promised Papa that she wouldn't fight anymore since the big scuffle she'd gotten in five years earlier that had ended up with her breaking her nose and her opponents battered enough to try to squeeze money from the family.

A promise was a promise, no matter how much time passed, so she whirled right back around and left the way she came.

Her heart was still thundering as she got into her truck, her fists wanting to bang against the dashboard in a fit. She had been so sure she was over her ex-husband and everything that had happened between them, but all it had taken was a single comment from a town drunk to make her feel so small and worthless again.

When would she ever be over it? When would she be able to think about what happened and not feel the horrendous squeeze of it? It was like he had planted himself in her soul, her first love, her first *everything*; he'd been the love of her life, but she hadn't been *enough,* and he'd run off to...

Her phone rang and she was tempted to throw it out the window. But the only people who called her was her family and lawyers, so she pulled it from her pocket to look at the screen.

Sure enough, it was Cass.

"Hey, I thought you said it was an extended appointment," she said as she hit the accept button, trying to sound calm and nonchalant.

"Huh? Oh. We're still going. I was actually calling for something else."

Something else? "What's going on? Is everything okay?"

"Whoa, calm down there, sis. I promise it's not a car accident every time; nothing super bad is going on. I was just calling to ask you a favor."

"...uh-huh?"

"Yah, remember that kid you drove here? The doctor's daughter, Savannah? Well apparently she missed her bus home and so Dr. Lumis is worried about her walking home alone. He's out on the phone with her now and I think they're arguing about her walking by herself, so before I volunteer you, I wanted to ask your permission."

It hadn't been what she was planning, but picking up the

precocious preteen would definitely be a good distraction from the sinking feeling in her gut.

"Sure, yeah. I can do it, no problem."

"Awesome! I'll go tell him now."

There was silence, then muffled voices going back and forth for a couple minutes, then suddenly the doctor was on the phone. Charity found herself flushing for a moment at the deep rumble of his voice, accent thicker than it had been in person. Was it because he was stressed? Worried? Or was it just something about the phone speaker's inability to catch the baritone of his voice?

"Hello, Miss Miller?"

"You can call me Charity. It'd be weird to call my sister and me the same thing."

"Right. Uh, Miss Charity. Your sister tells me that you wouldn't mind picking Savannah up and bringing her here? I would normally never ask, but she's been talking nonstop about the cool, cardplaying cowgirl she met, so I figured telling her that you were the one coming to pick her up would be plenty convincing to make her sit still."

"She the independent type?" Charity asked with a chuckle, her pride bubbling up at the thought that she was "a cool, cardplaying cowgirl."

"She has difficulty staying still. It's something we're working on."

Charity understood that. Back when she was younger, sometimes it felt like she was going to crawl out of her skin if she was forced to be still and quiet and not *do* something. She had an intense drive to be productive. To learn, to do, to make, to fix, to *create*. Some people just didn't get it. "I don't mind at all. I can be there in ten minutes."

"I can pay you, of course, for your time. I hope I'm not

crossing a boundary here, or that you feel like a ride share service—"

It was kind of cute how he was scrambling, so caught up between his need to be polite and his urge to take care of his daughter.

"It's fine. I don't mind. She's a good kid. Dangerously smart, but a good kid."

The relieved breath he let out had *such* a story behind it. "Thank you. I'll have your sister text you my number, and I'll call Savannah and let her know you're on your way. I'm sure she'll be thrilled."

"Sounds good. See you in about twenty, twenty-five."

"Thank you, again. I owe you."

"Nah. Like I told you, in this small town we look after each other."

Charity hung up with a grin, surprised at the sudden change in her mood, but she wasn't about to question it. Tucking her phone back in her pocket, she headed towards the school she hadn't been to in years.

She pulled up to the familiar pick-up area and sure enough, Savannah was there, bouncing from foot to foot. Her face practically lit up when she clearly spotted Charity's truck, and the girl vaulted in as soon as the door was open.

"Hi! Thanks for the ride."

"Whoa there, someone's full of excitement. Did you have a good day at school?"

"Uncertain. A lot of times things seem good at first, but then they're bad. But I'm... cautiously optimistic, I think the term is?"

"Hah, spoken like a true old soul. What's it like being a senior citizen so young?"

Savannah just grinned at her, buckling up. "I was born

eighty years old and I've been aging ever since. It's a hard life, but someone's gotta do it."

"You truly are a modern of our times."

"It's my cross to bear."

They shared a laugh and Charity once again marveled at the strange young woman in her truck as she drove away.

"So what's it like on the ranch?" Savannah asked.

"What do you mean?"

"What do *you* mean, what do I mean? I was born in San Diego. I want to know what it's like."

It was a fair question; Charity just wasn't used to teenagers caring about homestead life. "Well, we tend to work on an earlier clock, although we've kinda shifted it around in my family so everyone rises at their natural times."

"I... what?"

Yeah, that probably needed a better explanation. "We all used to wake up at four or five a.m. and get to working. But that was back when we had school and extracurriculars and still wanted to keep up on chores. Now, without school, it's more spread out.

"Clara is the earliest riser of all of us. She's never really been a good sleeper, so she gets up between four and six a.m. to tend to the chickens. We have an automatic door on their coop so they can peck around their yard for themselves, but she'll refill their feed if they need it and check their nests for eggs. She also turns on the drip irrigation for our raised garden, harvests things that do better being picked when it's still cool, then takes care of our goats." Charity glanced at Savannah as she pulled out of the school loop, sure that the young girl would be bored by hearing about something as banal as the Miller family schedule, but she seemed utterly enraptured by the information, staring with the intensity she'd had during Speed.

"Usually, by then, Charlie is up. He'll milk our four cows, put out food for the barn cats, then mostly yard work. His job is the most varied, between mowing, trimming back bushes and making sure that nettles don't grow in places they can hurt our animals. Then he'll work out or something, and usually goes horseback riding for a couple hours.

"Cass and I always used to get up at the same time and do a walkabout to help with any of the other chores our siblings didn't get to. Then usually it's running one of our machines, or doing maintenance, maybe even repairs on the house or barn. There's always something that needs fixing or shoring up. Or to be built. Those are my favorites. Especially since Papa's always expanding and improving his garden."

"He has a big one?"

Charity nodded. "We grow some crops for feed and for a contract with the two restaurants we have in this town, but his garden is all for us to eat from or share. Oh, and for our booth at the local corn festival every fall. He likes to grow a bunch of unique varieties that most people don't even know about."

"Isn't gardening a woman thing? That's what I always heard."

"Growing food isn't a gendered thing really. Everyone's gotta eat, right?"

Savannah nodded. "That makes sense. Just like my dad tells me I can be a doctor if I want, even though almost every doctor I know is a man."

"Oh yeah, there are plenty of women doctors."

"Yeah, just like there are tons of cowgirls too."

Ah, to have the conviction of a teenager. Charity remembered when she knew everything about the world and then some. She chuckled lightly, remembering when the world was black and white.

"Why are you laughing?" Savannah asked, and Charity could see in her peripheral vision that the doctor's daughter was squinting at her, tone reproachful.

"I'm not chuckling at you. I was just thinking of how when I was in high school and so certain of everything you could imagine. Sometimes I miss that girl."

Savannah nodded. "I've heard about that. I hope I'm not like that when I'm in high school, but everyone always says I'm already too smart for my own good."

Wait, something about that sentence didn't make sense. "What do you mean, when you're in high school? It's the new year, aren't you a freshman now?"

The girl blinked at her. "...I'm ten. I'm going to be eleven soon, though."

It took a remarkable amount of control to not slam her brakes. "You're *what?*"

Savannah tilted her head, as if she couldn't fathom Charity's shock. "I'm ten. Why does everyone act like that's so strange?"

Charity swallowed, trying to right that fact in her head. Savannah was *ten?* That seemed impossible.

"Is this why everyone thinks that I've failed a grade or two until I start talking to them? I don't understand it."

There was a layer of insecurity there, layered under her inquisitiveness. Charity picked it up right away and forced herself to get over her shock. "You're very tall for your age, Savannah. Add that to how you talk, it makes it seem like you're at least thirteen."

"...Oh, is *that* all it is?" she sounded relieved. "I thought it was another one of those things."

"Those things?"

Savannah nodded as if it was obvious. "Yeah, a thing. Like when people are making fun of me but they're smiling and being nice about it, so I can't figure out what they actually mean. They say it's sarcasm, but it's not. I *like* sarcasm. I think I might be good at it. But I can't tell what they're doing."

Charity knew exactly what she meant, and her heart ached. "No, it's nothing like that. You're just very tall and very smart. There's nothing wrong with that."

"Yeah. I'll probably end up taller than you. Maybe as tall as my dad. Apparently, my mom was his height and all of her brothers were waaay taller."

Was.

Was.

Charity was so familiar with that language that she didn't even have to ask. There was a certain lexicon that kids who lost a parent had to adapt, and it shined like a beacon to anyone who recognized it.

That explained why the doctor was so concerned about his daughter. If there was anything that could make fear bloom in someone's chest, it was losing a family member.

"That's awesome. All of my cousins are pretty tall too. My sisters and I are the only ones who are six feet and under."

"You're six feet?"

"No, but almost. Five-eleven. My middle sister, Clara, is six foot actually. I'll have to introduce you two sometime."

The girl perked up, all that melancholy from before falling away like only a kid could do.

Wow, a *kid*. Not a teenager. The revelation still kicked around the back of Charity's head.

"Really? Would you?"

"Of course. I don't see why not."

"And she's a cowgirl like you?"

"I... suppose. But she's always been more of a farmgirl, I think."

"What's the difference?"

"She'd have to tell you herself. She's always the one who makes the distinction."

"Okay. I'll put together a list of questions to ask her, so I don't forget anything."

"Oh, I'm sure she'd absolutely *love* that."

Savannah carried on, all whipped up in her excitement again, and it was utterly adorable. They were almost to the doctor's office, and Charity couldn't help but wonder if this was just what it was like to have a kid or if Savannah was an exception.

She hadn't figured out by the time they arrived, but as Savannah bounced out of her truck and skipped up to the porch without missing a breath, Charity was whisked away into a vision of what her family might have been if she'd had a kid. If Savannah was *her* ten-year-old, and not the child of the new town doctor.

Would she still be with her ex? Would he ever have strayed? Would he be waiting back at home to kiss her lips, spin her around, then pick up their child and ask them about their day? In a rush of colors, she saw birthdays that never existed. Holidays celebrated hand in hand. She saw their dream home being built together on the opposite end of Papa's land.

It was so sweet, layered in wonderful dreams that had occupied her mind ever since she was fifteen, and it hurt her more than a dagger into her heart.

Those teeth returned, vicious and ravenous, eager to rip her apart all the more.

Upset rose quickly and her eyes began to sting in that tell-tale way. She said some sort of excuse and hurried past Savannah, heading straight for the bathroom before any tears could fall. She needed to get herself together.

It'd been five years since everything was finalized. Why couldn't the pain just *stop*? It wasn't like she had an empty life. She purposefully engineered her days to be as busy as possible so she would never have too much time to stop and linger with her thoughts. With the black misery that loved to stalk her in the back of her mind.

Besides, she had her siblings and her Papa to worry about, and that should have been enough.

...but why did it feel like it wasn't?

7

———————

Alejandro

Alejandro heard Charity and Savannah before he saw them, pushing the exhausted Cass Miller out into the lobby. She'd done an amazing job in her session, but he'd had to stop her several times to tell her not to push herself too hard. She was a type A patient through and through, pushing herself harder than she should have.

Lots of people thought that being motivated was the tops. But there was a limit to it. Too many reps, pushing too hard, could increase injuries, delay healing, and make things so much worse. Type A patients had a hard time listening to their body and accepting that they had limits. He was going to have to keep a close eye on her.

"And these goats don't faint?"

Charity laughed and *wow*, was that a sound. Slightly husky, but open, full of brightness that he didn't quite expect from her. Not that the woman looked or acted like she was doomy or gloomy, but there was a certain seriousness to her. Maybe it was her catlike eyes, maybe it was her toned muscles on her broad frame, hips as wide as her easy smile.

"No, most goats don't faint, actually, that's just a very particular breed." He realized that the woman was showing his daughter videos on her phone, Savannah seemingly utterly enraptured.

"Why don't they have ears?"

"It's the breed they are, Lamanchas. They have ears, they're just tiny."

"Ah, that makes sense."

He cleared his throat and Savannah looked up; her face bright like it was whenever she found something new that excited that wonderful mind of hers.

"Dad!" she hollered, running to him and jumping into his arms. It'd been a while since she'd done that, but he still caught her and lifted her up. Too soon he wouldn't be able to. How was it his little girl always managed to grow so fast? Just yesterday she had been a toddler who cried and cried because her mommy didn't come home. "Can we go to the Miller Ranch? It's *sooooo* cool!"

He loved seeing his daughter so excited, but he couldn't help but feel embarrassed. He was a private sort of person, always had been, and his often-extroverted daughter tended to push him into more social situations than he would prefer.

"It's presumptuous to invite ourselves over to my patient's home, *miha*. Besides, I'm sure they're very busy on the ranch."

But then Cass Miller piped up, because of course she did. "Actually, we wouldn't mind at all. It's been a while since we've had kids there. I think... a year ago when some of our cousins visited? And their babes are all real young." There was a pause, and then Cass looked to her sister with a look that certainly meant *something* even if Alejandro wasn't sure of what. "Isn't that right, Charity?"

Another pause and the two were *definitely* having some sort of silent conversation before Charity shrugged. "Sure. I have some time on the weekend if you want to stop by. You can meet all of the goats you want."

Savannah let out a sound and booked it from where Alejandro had set her down over to Charity, throwing her arms around the woman. Alejandro stared, eyes wide, completely sideswiped by his daughter.

It wasn't that Savannah was anti-touch, but she wasn't the most trusting young kid. Too many bullies and people who had betrayed her confidence or mocked her whenever Alejandro wasn't there. He hadn't seen her just out-and-out hug a stranger like that since... well, since *ever*.

Who were these strange Miller sisters? One daughter who seemed like a relentless force and the other a mystifying one, both of them with long stories that he had no way of finding out. He had a rule of not looking up the personal details of his patients, even if the temptation was there. Seemed like a violation of their privacy.

"If you're sure," he said.

She shot him a crooked sort of grin that made his heart thump in his chest. What was *that* about? "I don't say things I'm not sure of."

"Right. Well. This weekend then. We can text the details later. I imagine you want to get your sister home."

"Yeah," Cass added, looking entirely satisfied. Alejandro wasn't sure why she seemed so pleased. "Your sister wants a hot soak before I curl into a stiff little ball. Let's get me home."

"I'll make you some of that fresh batch of chamomile tea while you're soaking. It'll help with the muscle pain."

"You make your own tea?" Alejandro asked, impressed that she knew chamomile was useful for muscle pain.

"Papa does, actually. He's taught us, but none of us can quite keep up with him, so it's mostly his." She tipped her head and Alejandro tried to catch up with that information. "I'll see you this weekend, Savannah."

"I'll see you, Charity! And you'll show me all of the things!"

"All of 'em. I promise."

Savannah practically vibrated as the two left, whirling back to him and ricocheting off the walls. Mrs. Whittaker returned from the bathroom, her eyebrows raising at his rocket of a daughter.

"Something good happen?" she asked, a sweet smile on her face.

"I hope so," Alejandro said, feeling his cheeks color. Three weeks in a new town and he was visiting his first neighbor's house. "I really hope so."

8

Alejandro

It was time to visit the Miller Ranch.

Alejandro gripped the steering wheel of his car more tightly, nerves sparking through his chest. Despite his personal motto of leaving privacy for his patients, Savannah had done some research and found out that the Millers were basically a ranching and agricultural empire built out of old money. It was intimidating and a bit worrying, to say the least.

Sure, Alejandro had money. More money than he'd ever had in his life. But he was raised poor, and both he and his wife had had to fight tooth and nail while he was going through medical school. They had scrimped, saved, denied themselves so many comforts because they both believed in their future together.

Now Alejandro had his future, but his beloved never got a chance to.

It was so unfair.

"I've never been on a ranch! Have you been on a ranch? Before I was born?"

Savannah's excited bouncing in her seat brought him back to the present, and he managed a smile. "No, *miha*. Can't say I have. Your mother and I went to a few wineries once or twice, but that's it."

"I can't wait. What do you think we'll see first?"

"One of the Millers, I imagine. How many of them did you say there were?"

"Six. The father and five children. Their mother died a long time ago."

Wait, *what*? Charity had lost her mother too? When she was young? Was she able to sense that about Savannah? Was that why the two had mysteriously clicked just like that? "You found all that out online?"

"Most of it was pretty easy. The mom part was easy because there was an article about the ten-year anniversary of the scholarship she has in her name for music students to go to this expensive college on the east coast, and it talked about her death. Something about Hunting Disease?"

"Huntington's?"

"Yeah, that was it."

Alejandro swallowed. That was... that was awful. Granted, cancer had taken his beloved, but somehow that didn't seem quite as horrifying. Still tragic, still a mother lost before her time. But Huntington's... there was no cure for that.

"Please don't bring that up in front of them."

Savannah was smart, but sometimes she didn't seem to understand what kind of things were rude or would upset other people. She never set out to be mean or insensitive, but sometimes she ended up there anyway. He supposed that was what happened when a kid was full of so much information but not enough age to discern what was private or not.

"Oh! Is that it? We're here!"

Sure enough, there was a gravel road leading away from the paved one, and a large archway that had a sign with the name *Miller* painted across it. Truly giant sunflowers were standing around it, taller than Alejandro. Some even taller than two Alejandros, although most of their heads were bowed from the sheer weight of their seeds. There were netted sacks over the drooping blooms, which he guessed was a way to keep birds and squirrels from making off with the treats.

Savannah's mother used to love ranch-flavored sunflower seeds. She would eat them by the pound and often would spoil her dinner if she wasn't careful. It was an inside joke of theirs, and one he hadn't thought of in a long, long while.

"That's *pretty*," Savannah remarked, plastering herself to the window.

"It is, isn't it?" Bittersweet on his tongue, but beautiful. Just like when he looked at Savannah and saw so much of her mother. "Let's remember our manners, alright?"

"I will. But Charity won't really care. She's cool like that."

"Cool or not, we still need to be polite."

Savannah nodded in that way of hers where he couldn't tell if she was listening or not, but he would just have to trust her. His daughter was a good kid; he knew she wanted to be good.

Driving under the arch, he followed the gravel road until it widened into a large and long driveway in front of a truly impressive house. Savannah was already making sounds of wonder and vaulting from his car, charging right towards what had to be the front door on the wraparound porch.

It was a mansion, that was for sure, but it was the least

mansion-y mansion that he had ever seen. Made of wood and cobblestone, with plenty of large, glass windows, it looked like someone had taken the idea of a humble cottage in the woods but made it *giant*. There were three floors, and the width of the building probably could have fit three of his entire practices next to each other.

Apparently, Savannah had *not* been exaggerating about their wealth.

The door opened and an older man stepped out. He was tanned, with a straw hat on. He was wearing sweats and a loose T-shirt, which surprised Alejandro. He wasn't sure why he'd expected the man to come out in overalls or cowboy boots, but he wasn't wearing anything like that.

"Ah, you must be Savannah," he said as Alejandro got out of his car. The man grinned, and Alejandro could recognize the features his daughters had inherited. Despite his crow's-feet and smile lines, the man's eyes were intense, and his jaw was strong and rugged looking. "I've heard a lot about you."

"Like what?" Savannah asked, grinning up at him.

"Mostly that I should never play you in Speed. Although I'm used to having the tar beaten out of me, considering I'm the only one who will still play Charity." The man looked up and beamed at Alejandro. Oh, yup, his daughters definitely got that beaming smile from him too. "Hi there. I assume you're the doctor?"

"That would be me, yes," Alejandro said, bounding up the steps of the porch to shake the man's hand. His grip was as strong and calloused as one might expect from a rancher, but his expression was wide and friendly. "Alejandro Lumis. I don't expect you to call me doctor."

"I'm Papa Miller, and the girls call you Doc enough that I'm afraid that's mostly stuck in my head."

The Miller sisters talked about him? What did they say?

Before he could wind himself around that thought too much, the door banged open, then Cass Miller was rolling onto the porch. She too was dressed in sweats, but that was normal considering she had worn loose and baggy clothing the two times he'd seen her.

Strange, to have only met both of the women twice and yet he was at their home. He wasn't the most sociable person, so he felt entirely out of his depth.

"Would you like to come in?" she asked, sending him a grin that was indeed identical to her father's.

"Of course. Your house looks lovely."

"Thanks! My dad built most of it with his buddies, but we've been adding onto it here and there. Charity just finished the solar panels a couple years ago."

"You have solar panels?" Savannah asked, bouncing after Cass as she effortlessly rolled in. That was when Alejandro realized there was a small, hardly noticeable ramp leading from the lip of the front door onto the open porch. And that there were two ramps leading from the porch to the ground, one on the far side and one right beside the steps he'd bounded up.

"Your house is very accessible," he said without thinking.

But Cass just laughed, seemingly pleased. "That's all Charity too. She needed something to keep her busy while I was in the hospital. She's a worrier." Alejandro blinked several times, taking in all the polished, professional additions, and Cass laughed again, but even harder. "What, you're surprised a woman made all of this?"

That had him coloring up his neck. He didn't want to be invited into their home and insult them or appear sexist. "No, of course not. I've just never been very good with building things or tools, so I assumed all of this would have been professionally made by contractors."

"Ah, don't worry about it. I was just teasing you. I forget that not everyone is used to my humor."

"Where *is* Charity?" Savannah butted in, shifting from foot to foot.

"Oh, Clara said that Charity had a hard time sleeping, so she's been out working on some sort of wheelchair accessible go-kart sort of thing out at the garage since before the sun came up."

"Why would you need that? You seem to move around okay."

"The ground is pretty uneven over certain parts and there's always the chance of me falling out of my chair. And a mobile scooter can't handle dips or holes. A couple years back my aunt in Wyoming broke her ankle or something in a gopher hole."

"That sounds scary."

"Just a part of ranch life. I don't think it's a big deal, but," Cass said and shrugged, "like I said, she's a worrier."

Alejandro had been so caught up in looking around, taking in the homey décor and the impressive amount of flourishing house plants, along with plenty of photos in different places, that he hadn't realized they'd made it next to a quaint, retro kitchen and Cass was pushing a cup of sweet tea into both his and Savannah's hands. He drank from it dutifully and was surprised to taste hints of lavender and honey. What was that Charity had said? Their Papa liked to make tea? Where had the man even gone?

Alejandro didn't know, because the patriarch was nowhere around as far as he could see.

"Would you like to go visit Charity in her garage?" Cass

asked Savannah, grinning. "You can distract her long enough so she won't yell at me for going over uneven ground."

"Yeah! I'm a great distraction! Sometimes my classmates ask me to bring up a complicated question to the teacher so we run out of our time for a pop quiz."

"That's... that's not a good thing, Savannah," Alejandro murmured.

But Cass just grinned again. "Man, where were you when I was in school?"

"Not even born yet. You're old."

"Fair enough. Let's go, shall we?"

They headed out of the house and down a dirt path that had clearly been worn by decades of people walking along it. They barely got around the side of the mansion when they were confronted by a truly *massive* garden.

There was a cute fence around it built out of wood painted in light and dark purple. There were four archway entrances —one on each side—that had roses growing all over the trellises. Inside were long, low raised beds that were absolutely teaming with life, as well as wire archways between half of them in different spots.

"You should see the garden when it's in it's prime," Cass said when she must have realized that both he and Savannah had stopped dead in their tracks. "Although Papa did plant a lot of his fall starts, most of our summer crops are winding down or we yanked 'em out."

"Fall garden?"

"Yeah, we've got a pretty long growing season here, so we have plenty of time for cooler weather plants. Besides, it's so hot during the summer that anything in the brassica family has a hard time growing in the thick of it."

Brassica family. Right. Because Alejandro knew what that was right off the top of his head. "I see."

"I'm happy to give y'all a tour later, but it'd have to be the afternoon. Now that it's cooler, Papa likes to get a lot of work done between eleven and dinner. It's best not to get in his way."

"Does he get angry?" Savannah asked, skipping over to Cass's side.

Alejandro watched Cass as subtly as he could, already noting that she seemed to be doing better with her chair and her stamina had improved. Excellent.

"Oh no, nothing like that. But if there's one thing Papa likes as much as his garden, it's talking. He'll end up telling you about something or other, and the next thing he knows, it's nearly sundown. So, we all try to respect his busy time." A fond sort of expression crossed her face. "We don't always do the best at that though, especially when we're all inside under the air conditioning in the middle of summer."

"He tells good stories then?"

"The best."

"I want to hear some."

"Stick around enough and I'm sure you'll get a chance to."

"Aw *yes!*" Savannah said, pumping her fist in a way that reminded Alejandro of exactly how young she was.

Eventually, they did pass the garden and continued along the path. The distinctive smell of animals and their droppings soon became pretty evident, then a barn and another small building came into sight, on opposite sides of the path. He had no idea what the smaller building could be, and why there was a fence around it, until he spotted a chicken strut out from behind it.

Oh, a chicken coop. Right. That made sense.

Alejandro couldn't help but be internally amused at himself. He'd been a city boy all of his life, but he had never thought of himself as a stereotype. But the more he saw of the ranch, the more he realized he knew almost nothing about the whole deal.

But it was fascinating, all of it. He could see why Savannah was so absorbed in the idea of it all.

"Where are the goats?" she asked excitedly, still bouncing away.

"They're on the other side of the barn where they have a big ol' yard to run in with our cows. The garage is actually kind of in the center of our layout, then the horses are beyond that."

"I wanna see *all* of it."

"All in good time. I'm sure Charity will be happy to show you whatever you want."

"I hope so. I like her."

"Don't worry. I assure you that the feeling is mutual."

Savannah nodded strangely and seemed to fall into her thoughts as they walked the rest of the distance to the "garage." Alejandro heard the place before he saw it, music blasting so loud he almost thought he was at a concert.

It was classic rock, loud and hard on the drums. Savannah clapped her hands over her ears, and Cass had to call out twice before Charity's head popped out into one of the two open car doors of the garage.

"Oh hey, you're here!" she yelled right back, reaching into her pocket and pulling out some sort of remote. With a click, the music stopped, and Alejandro could hear his own thoughts again.

Charity walked out, wearing oil-stained overalls and taking a large set of headphones off her ears. Of course,

Savannah was already bounding over to her, questions flying.

"Why did you have headphones on when you were already playing loud music?"

"Because I had to stop what I was doing and listen to a wiring tutorial on my phone." She held up the device then handed it to Savannah. "You can start it over from the beginning if you want to know what I was working on."

"Really?"

Charity shrugged again. "Sure, why not. I could always use another brain to pick."

"You're going to *what* my brain?"

"It's just a saying. I just mean it would be nice to bounce ideas off someone who knows what I'm talking about."

Savannah grinned brightly and Alejandro couldn't help but just stand back and enjoy the interaction. His daughter was outgoing, yes, she got that from her mother, but that didn't mean people were kind to her. Or that they liked her. But both of the Miller sisters seemed to genuinely enjoy his daughter's personality.

Alejandro didn't know why he found that so surprising. *He* thought his daughter was amazing, after all. He wouldn't change a single thing about her (except that whole growing older thing. Was there a way to pause that for a while until he was ready?), but other people certainly had... *opinions.*

He did his best to protect her from them, but there was only so much he could do when all it took was one errant or backhanded comment to destroy confidence in a young person. Especially a young person who didn't always understand what lines she was crossing or why people found her... odd.

"Hey, don't go trying to take my place now," Cass warned.

"I'm Charity's right-hand man and second-in-command. As soon as I get out of this chair, I can show you how she can't survive without me."

Savannah looked dubious, but the older sister just nodded. "It's true. Just don't say that to her face because her head will get even bigger."

"Excuse me," Cass said in what was clearly mock indignation. "I cannot help that you have a tiny head from coming out the birth canal first."

Savannah perked up at that, and Alejandro had to withhold a groan. Kids focused on the strangest things. "Is that true?" she asked, looking back at her dad.

"Normally only with twins where one is leaving the mother right after the other. The human body has remarkable healing abilities, and most women return to their standard equilibrium if they're given enough time between births. Provided there are no injuries or complications."

"Ah, I see. That's kinda scary but cool."

Maybe it was a little frank for a talk with a ten-year-old kid. Alejandro hadn't been planning on telling his daughter where babies came from or any sex ed until she was *at least* fourteen at the earliest. But he'd made the mistake once of hiring a babysitter who was more interested in her phone than Savannah, so his daughter had gone into his study and taken different textbooks of his to read every day after school. He didn't find out until she apparently had found one that had helped him through his OB-GYN rotation and *goodness*, had she had a lot of questions.

Alejandro had a strict policy about never lying to his daughter—too many people did that because they thought she wouldn't understand things—so he explained everything he thought was appropriate. That was back when she was eight, and occasionally she would field him a question that would let him know she was ready to understand more. She was aware that a baby came from a woman, and what gestation was, and other things like that, but thankfully she hadn't seemed to put together what it was people did to *put* the baby inside there. All Alejandro could do was pray he had a couple more years at least before she got around to asking that.

Sometimes, it was the strangest things that made being a single parent so hard.

"See?" Charity said. "Scientifically, I do not have a big head."

"Nope, only metaphorically. And back when you used to let your hair curl."

"You mean frizz? That was *not* a good look. Thank goodness puberty settled all that mess down."

"Do you have pictures?" Savannah said, bouncing around. "Your hair is so *long*. I would love to see it curly!"

"Uh... maybe some physical ones that we got developed back in the day."

"What ones that you got what-ted?"

Both sisters stared for a moment before Charity clicked her tongue. "I'm only thirty-two and yet somehow you just made me feel eighty years older."

Charity went on to explain how photos used to work while Cass chimed in naturally. Alejandro had never had any siblings himself, and it was quite entertaining watching the two. He wondered if all five were like that, or if it was just the two eldest.

"So when can I see your garage?" Savannah asked, craning her neck past Charity. "Is it like a... a... mechanic shop or something?"

"I wouldn't go so far, but I've got tools and projects in here.

Ask your father though, because some of the stuff is dangerous and you always need a parent's permission for that kind of thing."

Savannah looked back at him with such big eyes that he couldn't help his chuckle. "You can take a tour. Just keep your hands to yourself."

"Yay! Thanks!"

If Charity was surprised, she didn't say anything. She simply held out her hand and Savannah took it with a squeal, skipping along beside the tall woman as she walked into the garage.

"Two peas in a pod, aren't they?" Cass asked, rolling over.

Alejandro hadn't been expecting that statement, hadn't even really thought about it himself. But he still found himself nodding. "They sure are."

9
————

Charity

Alejandro stood at the door, lingering in the corner of her vision but otherwise letting her lead Savannah everywhere. Naturally, the girl had a dozen and one questions about every single thing around her. It probably should have been annoying, but Charity found herself endlessly amused by it—and maybe a little prideful. She liked to think that she didn't have the biggest ego, but it was so nice to have someone look at her like she was infinitely impressive.

Because compared to her cousins, both in Montana and Texas, she and her siblings were largely unremarkable. They didn't run rescues or rehabilitate veterans or set up massive charities that helped thousands. And they didn't have a mega-corporation with its fingers in everything.

Nope, the western Millers were the quaint ones of the

family. Happy to homestead and be together and maintain their wealth but not hoard it.

"Where did you learn to make all this stuff?" Savannah asked.

"The internet mostly, but I also took vocational classes in high school and did a couple apprenticeships around town."

"What are vocational classes?"

"It's not something they really seem to offer anymore, which is a shame. But they're classes that teach you about specific physical skills or jobs."

"Why did they get rid of them if they're so useful?"

"Beats me. I could say a lot about our education system, but I doubt you want to hear about that."

But Savannah nodded gravely. "They don't like the way I learn, a lot of the time."

"They who?"

She made a vague gesture. "I don't know. The schools? Or whoever handles the, uh, education. Like... the Education Government? Or... or... something about wooden education?"

It didn't make sense for Charity's heart to surge with a strange sort of warmth. "Do you mean the board of education?"

Savannah beamed at that. "Yeah! You get it."

"I do, I think."

"So, what's that?"

She pointed and Charity continued to explain. Somewhere in the back of her mind she was aware that it wasn't usual for a kid to want to hang out with an adult she'd only met twice and vice versa, but that was exactly where they were.

Before she knew it, quite a bit of time passed, and her throat was sore from talking. She paused to get everyone drinks from the fridge in the corner of the garage, Savannah making a face at the plain water but drinking it anyway. But as things wound down, Charity found she didn't want Savannah to go.

She expected Alejandro to say something about leaving. After all, he'd been largely silent the whole time, just watching while leaning against the doorframe, hands in his pockets. If it wasn't for the soft smile on his face and hazy look in his eyes, she would have thought he was bored out of his mind.

But no, he seemed genuinely happy to see his little girl happy. She couldn't help but wonder at his and his child's story. What had made these lovely but very city folk come to their small town. If they still felt the scars of losing someone who was supposed to be with them for decades more. But that wasn't exactly polite conversation for the third time meeting someone who was also her sister's doctor.

"So, you want to see the goats?" Charity asked when she was done draining her water bottle and went to grab another.

It was like she'd asked the girl if she wanted to *fly*. Savannah clapped her hands and jumped up and down. "Goats! Goats! Goats! *Goats!*"

"I'll take that as a yes. Come on. Watch your feet though. It's kinda easy to roll your ankle if you're not paying attention."

And just like that, Savannah's hand slid into hers like it was the most natural thing. And it certainly felt that way. Charity knew it had no right to. Savannah was only one step away from a stranger and *ten*. But they clicked. Like they'd always known each other.

Or maybe Charity was just lonely.

Tucking that thought away for another time, she led

Savannah to the goats, Alejandro following along behind them and Cass having gone inside at least an hour earlier.

As it turned out, Savannah *loved* goats.

She was high enough energy that it took extra time for most of them to warm up to her, but Borneo, their most rambunctious buck, absolutely loved her. The pregnant gals who were all kidded up for their fall births were much more cautious, but after a quick tutorial of how to approach and talk to them, they all accepted Savannah and milled about.

Of course, it helped that Clara made sure all of their goats were very socialized. She was always the busiest during kidding season, where she would spend an hour or two in their pen every morning and every evening, just picking up the new babes, holding them, then putting them down in addition to all the milking, feeding and brushing. Naturally that made her all of the goats' favorite, but they liked the other Miller siblings well enough.

And Savannah too, apparently.

The sun began to sink, putting the light directly into their eyes, and Charity's stomach rumbled, reminding her that the only lunch she'd eaten was a protein bar from her snack case in the garage. Pulling her phone out, she realized it was already just past six, which meant either Papa or Clara had probably cooked dinner already and had it waiting inside the house for her.

She couldn't eat now. After all, it would be rude to have food in front of Alejandro and Savannah without offering them anything. And she wasn't ready to end her time with them yet. But her stomach was beginning to pinch and burn, so the mature thing would be to politely dismiss them and tell them she'd see them at Cass's appointment the next week.

...or she could invite them to dinner.

"Y'all hungry?"

Alejandro opened his mouth like he was going to answer, but Savannah beat him to the punch. "I'm *starving*. You got good stuff to eat? Dad can cook, but he's usually too tired to make anything complicated."

Her gaze slid to Alejandro, who seemed to be blushing ever so slightly on those stately cheekbones of his. How was someone who was so roguishly handsome also so incredibly cute at the same time?

"We have burritos and quesadillas more often than we probably should," he said.

"That sounds delicious to me," Charity said before wiping her hands on her pants. "I'm not the best cook, but my sister and Papa are, so I can pretty much guarantee something yummy if you're in for some country cookin'."

Charity extended her cleaned hand and just like that, Savannah grabbed it again, practically leaning into her side. "I'm game! Let's *gooooo*."

Alejandro gave her an apologetic, somewhat sheepish look and there was that feeling again, so warm and fuzzy inside of her. She sent him what she hoped was an assuring grin, and they all headed in.

"Hey everyone, I invited our guests to dinner. Hope y'all don't mind?"

"Did you?" a voice floated from the kitchen. "I hoped you would! I'll be right there!"

"It's okay, Clara," Charity called, pausing to pull her boots off and put them on the tall shoe rack with their thick mud mat below it. Grabbing her house slippers, she looked to the two with her. "Shoes off, please, since you're going to be staying. We have spare house shoes all along the top rows, so just pick something that feels comfy."

"You have a bunch of extra shoes for guests?" Savannah asked, leaning back to see the upper shelves. The shoe rack was almost as tall as Charity, so she couldn't quite blame her for the exaggerated stretch.

"I have a lot of cousins and they like to visit in batches. We also have a whole box of these slippers in our storage closet."

"*Whoa*," Savannah said like that was the most fascinating thing.

The two of them went about politely changing their shoes. Almost as soon as they were done, there were quiet footsteps and suddenly Clara appeared with a tray in her strong hands.

"Hello, lovely to meet you," she said with a sweet smile. "I'm Clara. My older sisters have told me all about you."

"You know, I keep hearing that," Savannah said, scampering over and taking one of the cups on the tray and looking excitedly at the pitcher. "What is this?"

"It's lavender lemonade. I've been in a purple sort of floral mood lately."

"I've never had lavender lemonade."

"Well, it's the perfect time to try then, isn't it?"

"Okay." Savannah held up her cup and Clara did something impressive where she shifted the tray to one hand and picked up the pitcher with her other, pouring a small bit in the cup for the young girl.

Charity had known plenty of picky kids growing up, so she was impressed by how game Savannah was at trying new things. Alejandro had to be a good father, to have a daughter who felt safe enough to take risks and experience things alien to her.

And sure enough, Savannah smacked her lips after several deep gulps. "It's good! Can I have more?"

"Of course, as long as you don't spoil your dinner."

"Don't worry," Alejandro said, his voice that same low, pleased rumble. "She's a fantastic eater."

Goodness, Charity needed to record him and play it on nights she and Clara both had trouble sleeping.

"It's because I'm so tall and I won't stop growing," Savannah said after drinking more. "Gotta feed my bones."

Clara laughed, her ruby lips parted in that happy, serene smile she seemed to wear whenever she had new people to feed. Charity hadn't been kidding about how much her middle sister loved cooking.

"Makes sense to me," Clara said. "Come now, I'll set you spots at our table."

"You're really pretty," Savannah said as they walked along, apropos to nothing. "And really *tall*."

Another peal of laughter and Charity had to repress a snort. Not because Clara wasn't beautiful, but because Clara was the first one to deny it. Out of the mouth of babes and fools...

"Goodness, aren't you sweet?"

"No, not really. I'm nice, but people say I talk too much to be sweet. Why are you wearing that dress? You look like some of the movies I watch. Do you watch older movies? In black and white?"

It was all that Charity could do not to gloat and reinforce Savannah's insistence that Clara was a work of art. By far the calmest and most even keel of all the siblings, it was probably a good thing Clara got the broadest Miller frame.

She was a big woman, just a shave over six feet tall and with strong, capable shoulders. She was a fairly accomplished seamstress, if only because she'd had to alter most of the dresses she liked to buy just to make them fit her properly. Then, puberty *really* hit her in high school. It became impossible for her to find clothes both tall enough for her and big enough to fit her all over without looking like parts of her were going to bust out. So she'd gone on to making her own clothes entirely.

There were probably people who thought Clara was ugly because she was both tall and heavy-set, but those people were clearly blind. And Charity wasn't just speaking from a bias—okay, maybe she was a *little* biased—but Clara was a glimpse of classic beauty, curvaceous and statuesque with bright eyes and full lips. She had the Miller frame and cheekbones, but her mother's eyes and skin, looking more like a doe-eyed beauty rather than having the intense gazes of all her siblings and most of her cousins.

"I *do* watch some of those movies. But I don't think I'm much like them."

"I would disagree," Alejandro said from behind Charity. "Have you seen *Some Like it Hot*?"

Clara stopped, turning to regard the doctor over her shoulder. "Are you comparing me to Marilyn Monroe?" she asked softly, and Charity didn't miss the spots of color growing on her cheeks.

Alejandro's tone was just as rumbling as he answered, making something twist in Charity's belly. "Well, the hair's darker, but otherwise I would say yes."

"Goodness... Charity, feel free to invite your friends to dinner whenever you want."

"...uh-huh."

Was she feeling jealous? That was silly. Shoving it out of her mind, she followed her sister to the table and then helped her in the kitchen as the rest of the family strolled in and settled.

The meal was excellent, really, and Charity's stomach was

happy to have delicious food in it. But she wasn't the only one who thought it was tasty, with Savannah exclaiming over it multiple times, declaring that she was coming over for dinner *forever*. And then Alejandro looked at her, his dark eyes wide, and declared that it really was good and that she was an excellent cook.

The two proceeded to have a warm, wonderful conversation where Clara invited him over whenever he wanted and even to teach him recipes if he had the energy on the weekend. Savannah championed that thought beside him, asking for seconds and then thirds. Alejandro was right; she was a fantastic eater.

Charity sat back from it, a smile on her face, but something ugly was curling in her. She *liked* people complimenting Clara, who was usually so content fading into the background and being a mediator for her siblings whenever tempers flared too much. She *liked* people being nice to her siblings. And yet with every compliment, with every friendly smile, her stomach sank further.

Because how could she ever compare to her sweetest sister? Clara was calm and kind, and it was clear that Alejandro was more introverted than his daughter. She was exactly the type a busy, widower doctor would need, young and strong and kind.

Charity wasn't anything like that.

She was all edges and rough fingers. Chapped skin and hangnails. She was covered in dirt as often as she was covered in manure, and that wasn't even mentioning sweat.

She knew she was getting ahead of herself, but it was so easy to see Clara in an apron in the doctor's kitchen, kissing his cheek as he returned from work and serving him an amazing dinner.

Charity was aware she was letting her imagination go too far. The doctor wasn't going to run off with her sister any more than he was going to run off with *her*. He was just a guest, staying for dinner, and she was getting carried away with the warm and fuzzies. She was just lonely, that was all, and had forgotten what it was like to be around people she hadn't known from birth.

So, she stomped down on the silliness and told herself to get it together. She wasn't a high school girl who needed to crush over the nearest attractive, non-related man. Ugh.

The meal ended on a pleasant note, of course, with Charlie and Papa excusing themselves along with Cass. The only one missing was Cici, who was back at college and no doubt kicking butt on the dean's list. Naturally Clara packed up to-go containers for their guests and packed them into one of her extra baskets. Clara *loved* giving people things in baskets or harvesting in baskets, and she had a truly impressive collection of them that she ordered whenever she found a sale or purchased outright every year at the corn festival.

"This was amazing! Can I come over next weekend too?"

"Don't you want to hang out with any of your new friends that are your age?" Charity asked. Not that she didn't want Savannah to be around, but she was still a bit sore over the jealousy that had been trying to take hold in her chest.

"What friends could I possibly have?" the girl said, much more sharply than Charity had expected. "I just moved here, and I don't like talking to new people because they call me a know-it-all. I'll make friends eventually, but... I don't know, I don't like to rush it."

Whew, that was a lot. Charity felt a twinge of sympathy for the girl and then her mouth was moving all on its own. "You can come over anytime your daddy says it's alright. Just let me know an hour ahead of time to make sure I'll be home, okay?"

Savannah nodded, grinning again, and then Alejandro was stepping forward.

"Thank you," he said, tilting his head, and *wow*, those eyes were heady and dark, pulling her attention to them like a lightning rod. "Is there anything I can do to repay you? I haven't seen Savannah have this much fun in ages."

"Please, no. I don't mind at all. This has gotten me out of my shell for a while. I have to be careful, otherwise I might just actually turn into a hermit one day."

"You'd certainly be the most attractive hermit I've ever heard of."

Wait.

What?

Alejandro's cheeks colored and she watched his Adam's apple bob as he swallowed. "Come on, Savannah, let's go home. Thank you all again."

He strode quickly out, Savannah waving the whole time, leaving Charity to stand there and blink after them.

It was just a compliment. That was all. He'd complimented Clara too and way more. She needed to get herself together and stop being desperate.

Sighing, she rubbed her face and headed in.

10

———

Charity

"**O**kay. Now loop the rope like I showed you... then you're done!"

Savannah jumped up, pumping both of her fists in the air. "I did it! I roped a calf!"

"That you did. It's more complicated to rope a full-sized animal, but you can wait until you grow up for that too."

"And I can do it on a horse?"

"Sure, if you want to learn how to ride a horse, that can come after."

Charity hadn't taught someone how to do any sort of rope-work since Cici was quite small, and it was nice to spend the entire afternoon walking Savannah through it. She was enthusiastic, and she absorbed information like a sponge. She asked interesting questions too, ones that none of Charity's other siblings had ever thought to mutter.

"Aw yeah! I'm gonna be the world's first doctor-astronaut-cowgirl!"

Charity laughed, because how could she not? "That's quite the ambition you have there."

"I know, but I figure I might as well dream big while I can. Most adults don't seem to be able to. I think it's bills. Bills seem terrible."

"Oh, they definitely are for most people. But you're right—let's not talk about bills. How about we go grab some popsicles and sit on the porch?"

"Aw *yeah!* That sounds great!"

"Alright, well let's untie Moo-rybeth, who has been such a good girl for us."

"Right, right. That makes sense. How do I do that again?"

Charity showed her and she picked it up like a champ, then they walked back to the house. It was a Saturday afternoon, so Clara was in the kitchen excitedly making supper for Savannah—and Charity expected a cake too—and Papa was in his garden. Charlie was off with his friends from the next town over at the quarry, and if she had to guess, Cass was probably sleeping.

So, the house was quiet as she headed into the kitchen, and Clara kissed her cheek as she passed Charity two ice pops made from the lemonade from yesterday, mixed with apricot juice. It was a tart, sweet mixture and Charity was sure that Savannah would like it.

They sat on the porch, quiet for a while, and she was happy to see that the young girl did indeed enjoy the popsicle, saying it was better than anything her dad used to buy in the store. And then there was that flicker of pride again, warm in her chest. But there was more than that, and after a moment's thought, she realized that she just liked seeing Savannah be happy. The girl deserved it.

"Why don't you think I'm annoying?"

Well, wasn't that out of left field? "Why would I think you're annoying?"

"Because I'm a motormouth. I ask too many questions. Because I always have to be doing something. Take your pick."

All of those things definitely sounded like stuff *other* people had told her, not things that she actually thought about herself, and Charity's heart squeezed. "I don't think you're annoying at all, Savannah. I like how much you talk. I like that you're enthusiastic and you always have so much to say."

"I... thanks. I like you too. You know so much cool stuff and you're nice."

"Well, I try to be."

There was quiet for another moment, but Savannah must have been in a blurting sort of mood because her next question was just as much of a non sequitur.

"So, I've met your Papa Miller twice now, but never a Mama Miller."

"Uh-huh," Charity said cautiously.

"Did you lose your mom too?"

"Yeah, yeah I did."

"When?"

"A long time ago."

"What happened? I mean, I looked it up online. I know she had Huntington's. But what I mean is... what was it *like*? Was it..." The girl swallowed hard, and it was so easy to see herself sitting there instead. "You're so brave, and you seem to know everything. But... was it scary?"

It wasn't something Charity usually liked to discuss. There

was certainly plenty of pain around that topic, a bone-deep sort of ache. But she wanted to share. Because if she could show Savannah that *she* had survived it, that she grew up to be okay, maybe it would give the girl more ammunition for all the troubles she was going to have to face.

"Yeah, she had Huntington's. She was normal, and then she started to get headaches, then she started to forget a lot. By the time we realized that something was wrong and took her to the doctor, we didn't have a lot of time left. She slid away in pieces, sometimes little bitty chunks, sometimes huge patches of her would be gone, and there was no way to tell which would happen.

"By the end, she couldn't do much of anything and there wasn't a lot of her there. It was kind of like watching her become a ghost, except she wasn't quite dead yet. She was just... fading."

Savannah nodded, her face serious. "It was kind of like that with Mom too, I think."

"You think?"

"I didn't really know her. Not well. I remember her being there. I remember her singing to me and feeling safe. I... I think I remember her smile. But I was somewhere just past two when she died. I don't even think I understood what death even was or that she was really gone for a long while. I don't exactly have a ton of memories from then.

"Sometimes I feel bad about it, like I should hurt more. And sometimes I feel nothing, because I can't even remember who I'm supposed to miss. And then I feel guilty because my dad... my dad loved her so much and he's still *so* hurt. He won't talk about it, most of the time, but I know. And I can't help but think that he's so *lonely*, but I don't really know what to do about it.

"Is he supposed to date? Am I supposed to help him find a new stepmom for myself? Is it bad that I don't want to share him with anyone? It's been just us for so long, I can't imagine anything else. But at the same time... I don't know if just him and me is enough. I want him to be happy like he makes me happy. I think I remember when he used to be happy, but he hasn't been, not really, since my mom died."

"That's a lot for a kid to handle."

"I think that it's a lot for anyone to handle."

"Fair point."

Savannah nodded, falling quiet for a while. It was pretty obvious to Charity that the young girl was thinking, and she felt herself falling into her own thoughts.

She thought that she had had it bad when she found out the love of her life was cheating on her. She thought she had it the worst when he tried to squeeze her family dry of money and extort her from millions during their messy divorce. But she would rather go through that all over again than watching anyone she loved slowly succumbing to an illness that ravaged their body and left them a shell of their former self. Watching their days become more and more painful as their energy sapped.

"I'm sorry, love. I wish I could say it gets better, and it does, but your and my situations are a little different. I was a pre-teen when my mom left, so I remember her. There isn't any ambiguity with us."

"What's ambiguity?"

Oh, right. Charity had forgotten just how incredibly young Savannah was. "It means, uh, open to different interpretations, kind of wishy-washy."

"So, nebulous?"

Of course, Savannah would know nebulous but not ambiguity. "Yeah. Nebulous."

"It does make me feel better that you understand though, even if your situation was a little different."

"No problem. I'm not the smartest person around, but I am the eldest of five siblings, so I learned quite a lot from just helping to raise us all." Despite the soft, sad smile on her face, Charity could still see the pressure pulling down at Savannah's shoulders. She needed a distraction so her young, still-forming brain could process all that was going on inside of that incredible head of hers. "Hey, you want to go meet a pony that would probably be *just right* for you to ride?"

Savannah practically choked on her ice pop as she whirled.

"Do I wanna *what?*"

"I'll take that as a yes. Come on."

Hand in hand, they jogged off together.

11

Alejandro

Apparently, corn could have its own festival.

When Alejandro had first moved to town and heard Cassidy Miller and Mrs. Whittaker talk about the "corn festival," he'd thought it was a nickname, or a joke. Later he thought maybe it was some sort of potluck.

But nope. It was a real, honest-to-goodness festival where most of the town was shut down and the main street was lined with different tents. It was quite an affair, that was for certain, and he hadn't realized just how much of a to-do it was until Savannah dragged him there.

"Wow! Is this a carnival?" Savannah asked, bouncing along beside him.

"Almost. Less hazardous rides, but fried food and I think I see a ring toss booth down there."

"Ooooh! I wanna ring toss, Dad! Can we go there!"

"Sure, we'll make our way down, but let's see what's on our way there."

"And maybe buy junk food?"

"And maybe buy junk food." He could smell the distinct scent of funnel cake in the air as well as other fried treats. While Alejandro generally didn't have much of a sweet tooth, he did have a soft spot for fair treats. There was just something inherently joyful about them.

Also, there was a very small list of things he wouldn't do for homestyle fried okra. He could *destroy* a plate of that in seconds flat.

They walked up to the first tent and saw pretty paintings, the artist an older woman with comically thick glasses. Alejandro bought something he thought would look nice in his office, a pretty landscape, and then they moved on.

The next tent had homemade jams, and he absolutely bought up several jars of that. Peach, red chili, prickly pear, mango pepper, then some classics like strawberry and blackberry. The young woman there seemed quite happy with his purchase of eight different jars and gave him a heavy, supportive canvas bag to haul his find.

"Dad," Savannah said as they stepped out. "Didn't you always teach me to walk around once before buying anything?"

"You're not wrong," he said with a wry grin. "But I'm planning to support almost all of these stands that I can." They entered the next one where they found *custom fresh salsas.* "Especially if they're all so *delicious.*"

He spent... much more money than he should. But with pineapple salsa, mango salsa, fresh salsa verde, roasted green chilis... it was a veritable smorgasbord.

Alejandro had learned how to make salsa when he was

young, of course, but he wasn't the best at it and he didn't often have the time to prep the tomatoes, roast all the ingredients, then actually can it. So when he had a chance to buy a year's worth of homemade, delectable salsas in a variety of flavors, well he was going to do it.

It wasn't until he was trying to cram the ten jars of salsa into his bag with the eight jars of jam that he realized he might have forgotten something important.

"You wanna borrow my cart?" the man behind the table asked, chuckling lightly.

"Oh, I couldn't," Alejandro said, feeling his cheeks color.

"You're the town Doc, right? My wife has an appointment with you next week. You can just give it to her when she comes in."

Huh, Charity was right. Small towns really did look out for each other.

"I would appreciate it greatly. I didn't quite count on there being so much here."

"You haven't seen anything yet. We've got a lot of crafty people here. And make sure you check out the Millers' stand. They basically give products away for free and they grow the most interesting things."

"I'm familiar with the Millers," Alejandro answered with a smile. Savannah spent almost every Saturday for the past three weeks at their ranch, and Alejandro had visited again with her. During that time, Papa Miller had indeed taken them on a garden tour and showed them some of the more exotic things he was growing. "Lovely family."

"That they are. Our town has certainly benefited since their Papa moved here. I remember my parents weren't quite sure what to think about them at first, since they were clearly rich, but it didn't take long for them to integrate. 'Course it helped that they instantly donated enough to fund all of the school's extracurricular programs for four years."

Alejandro nodded. So the Millers really were as fantastic as they seemed. Huh.

"Anyways, you enjoy yourself now!"

"Thank you, we'll try our best."

Pull-handle of the cart in one hand and Savannah's in his other, Alejandro strode along. The sun was finishing setting, but stringed lights between all the tents lit up, shimmering like stars. It was beautiful, in a simple, country way, and Alejandro couldn't help but stop, looking at the twinkling all around him.

It was like being in a fairy's circle, or some other enchanted place. It felt otherworldly and mystical, something too good for mere mortals. And yet there he was, with his daughter. He'd moved two months ago, and he never would have guessed he would wander into such a scene.

"Come on, Char, aren't you tired of cleaning us out every year?"

"First of all, only my family calls me Char. Secondly, absolutely not. It's a time-honored tradition to clean your booth out every year and I'm not ending that now."

Alejandro turned to the familiar voice, surprised to see Charity and two of her siblings at a tossing game, a comically large pile of stuffed prizes at their feet.

Charity tilted her head back, laughing after the guy at the stand sent her a rude gesture that was obviously in jest, and she looked *beautiful*. Not that she wasn't always attractive in a somewhat intimidating way, but there were spots of color bright on her cheeks, her hair was piled high atop her head in a braided, fancy bun, and she was dressed in a rockabilly sort of dress with matching reddish cowboy boots.

"Oh! It's Charity!" Savannah said excitedly, pointing. "Let's go say hi!"

His daughter practically vaulted over to Charity, throwing her arms around the woman in a very enthusiastic hug.

Clearly the move surprised Charity because she fell back a step, arms flailing and dumping her drink on the person walking behind her.

Oh no.

"I'm *so* sorry," she said, pulling herself out of Savannah's embrace and whirling to the person behind her.

"Watch where you're going," the man snapped, his words slurred, and Charity let out a curse.

"Of course, it had to be *you*. Look, Butch, I'm sorry. I didn't mean to. Let me buy you a drink, okay?"

"You think just because your family owns the most land around here that you can just treat us like peons?"

"No, of course—"

"You and your siblings there have a lot of gall coming down here, mingling with us low folk. You like laughing at us?"

"Geez, you're really taking that last verbal spat we had to heart. I'm sorry for spilling my drink on you. I'll—"

"Shut up. Just shut up. Your dad may have bought off half the town by throwing around all that money after your mom kicked the bucket but—"

The visceral reaction of Charity's body was unmistakable. Her spine snapped straight, and Alejandro felt like he could sense the heat radiating from her even from where he was.

"You are so lucky I promised my father I wouldn't fight anymore," she hissed, body rigid.

"Oh yeah? What you gonna do, cowgirl?"

Suddenly her brother was surging forward, quick as a flash. "She may have made a promise, but I sure didn't."

And then he slugged the guy right across the face.

Alejandro dropped the handle of his cart and rushed forward, trying to help, trying to get them to stop, he didn't know. More people were already surging forward, and he didn't know if they were friend or foe.

But what he did know was that, once he got close enough, he felt someone clock him right across the jaw.

Huh. He'd never been much of one for a fight anyway.

12

———————

Charity

*E*mbarrassed didn't even come close to describing how Charity felt. Her cheeks were on fire and she wanted to crawl into a hole. Or sink into the ground. Or hop on her horse and just disappear forever.

But she wasn't doing any of those things. Instead, she was holding an ice pack to Alejandro's jaw with beer spilled down her front, her knuckles scraped raw, and sweat cooling between her shoulder blades.

The things that he had to think about her! He'd seen her brawl like a delinquent on the street, punching and kicking and even biting at one point.

She hadn't meant to. She *really* hadn't meant to. Even when he'd said that horrible, awful thing about her mother, she remembered her words to her father.

But then Charlie had gone and started a fight, and then

Butch's crummy friends jumped in, and she wasn't about to let her little brother get beaten to a pulp. So she'd broken her promise and brawled along with her siblings.

It wasn't until about halfway through that she even realized that Alejandro was there, trying to pull someone away. A deep bruise was on his chin and guilt had swamped her. Suddenly, she had to defend both her brother and the doctor, and that was the last thing she had planned for.

"Are you alright?" she muttered finally. Everyone was separated and the town's cops knew them all enough to just lecture them and dismiss the crowd, so she knew she *should* say something, but with the whole aforementioned sinking into the floor thing, she didn't exactly have a whole lot to say.

"I'm... okay," he murmured quietly, his eyes flicking to her then back out at the mess that they made of the street.

He had to be thinking the worst things about her, and he *definitely* wasn't going to let his daughter come hang out at the ranch anymore. She'd single-handedly ruined both her image in his eyes but also Savannah's one big getaway from the realities of her life.

But to her surprise, he kept talking. "You have a pretty good hook there."

She felt herself blush all the way down her neck. "You noticed that, huh?"

He nodded, then winced when the movement pressed his chin into the icepack. "Yeah, I did. Thank you, you know. For getting me out of there. I wanted to help, but I guess I'm used to the healing part of things."

"I dunno, you only got hit once. You did better than Charlie."

He huffed the gentlest, softest laugh and Charity felt her

heart flutter. Gosh, she really was playing the idiot, but she felt like she couldn't stop sliding into it.

"And then my dad rushed in and he was like 'oh no you don't' and *kicked* the man through a tent!"

Savannah's bright voice drifted over from where she was telling Papa a very embellished story of the fight. It was clear that Alejandro heard her too, because he chuckled.

"She always sees the best in me."

"I get why," Charity said before she could think better of it. Uh-oh. Quickly she scrambled to say something else. "But it wasn't a big deal. Butch is a drunk and one of Eric's oldest friends. His whole old gang is always looking for ways to cause me trouble."

"Who's Eric?"

Uh, she really was batting a zero, wasn't she?

"It's not important. Just small-town drama."

"And here I thought folks in small towns look out for each other."

"We do, but that doesn't mean that there aren't some parts that are a bit like a soap opera. Are you okay to hold this? I don't think I can feel my hand anymore."

He nodded, but his hand came up more quickly than she expected and pressed against the back of hers.

His palm was warm, and surprisingly soft. The contact jolted through her like a shock, and she felt herself stiffen as he gently gripped her hand, moving it so that her knuckles were in his sight. She stood silently, feeling like her heart was about to explode as he examined them.

"I think you'll be alright, but make sure to clean those for me, okay?" His voice was so low, *so* low, barely a rumble and yet it rattled through her like a roar.

Charity had always been single-minded. Maybe even stubborn. But something about how he said it made her want to do whatever he asked of her.

"For you?" she found herself saying dazedly.

The heady, half-lidded expression he had vanished as he seemed to realize the implication of his words. "I'm the town doctor. It's my nature to care about everyone's health."

"Right. Of course." What else could he have meant?

They fell into silence as everyone wrapped up what they were doing. Clara was tending to Charlie's split lip and his black eye, which was fairly hard to do considering he was chiming in every other minute to Savannah's increasingly dramatic story.

Goodness, she loved her little brother.

It would have made her sick to let Butch talk about her mother like that, to insult her memory. But she also felt trapped by her promise to her father, especially since she only made it because he told her how much it scared him whenever she fought. How he was afraid he was going to get a call one day and he'd have lost her too.

She remembered it clearly, even though it was when she was just seventeen years old. And that was when she'd sworn to him that she'd never fight again unless it was in self-defense. It wasn't that Charity liked violence, but she understood that it was the only language some people spoke. Butch was one of those, and hopefully Charlie's punches would encourage him to leave her alone.

But considering how Charity had jumped in and gotten a few hits of her own while defending both Charlie and Alejandro... well, that was less than likely.

"Do you think it's too late to look at the rest of the tents?" Alejandro asked, a wry grin about those lips of his. Lips that she shouldn't pay so much attention to, but she stared at anyway.

When was the last time she kissed anyone? It had been Eric, hadn't it? The day before she'd found out exactly what he'd been up to when he was supposed to be establishing his new business with her seed money.

The day before her world fell apart for the second time.

"I think most everyone closed up to watch the festivities. If there's one thing a small town loves more than an obscure festival based on crops, it's a good ol' brawl. But this place will open back up tomorrow like nothing happened except for the hot gossip that's sure to go around." She gave Alejandro the best easy-going shrug she could. "Who knows, you might get a few patients from this who want to see the hot doctor that threw himself into harm's way to try to defuse a fight."

He chuckled at that and it was *such* a good sound. One that didn't make her feel nearly as embarrassed about letting that side of herself out again. She thought he'd be admonishing, or even angry that she'd exposed his daughter to such violence. But instead he seemed almost... admiring?

No. That couldn't be right. She was just seeing what she wanted to see, and she couldn't deny that she really, *really* wanted him to see her in a good light.

"Hey, Dad!" Savannah chirped, skipping up with a big, bright grin on her face. Charity had a feeling that she and the young girl were going to have a talk about how fighting was *not* the first solution to go to. Even if sometimes people had real punchable mouths that liked to say punchable things. "Is Charity's hand hurt?"

"What?"

"Huh?"

Both Charity and Alejandro spoke at the same time, their

heads whipping to the side, and it was only then that she realized the doctor was still holding her hand, his fingers warm and smooth compared to her worn ones. His palm broad, able to dwarf hers completely, but without any of the scars or wear and tear that came from ranching life.

"Don't worry, I have a clean bill of health," Charity said, opening her arms in a hug. "Didn't take more than a glancing blow."

"Yay!" Savannah ran forward into a hug that Charity was now familiar with. While the young girl wasn't as tactile as, say Cass was when she was younger, she still was an affectionate kid who liked her hugs and hair ruffled occasionally. Or at least that was what Charity had observed so far. That could change entirely once the girl became a teenager.

"Are you okay, Dad? I thought you didn't like fighting."

"I don't," Alejandro said with another one of those low laughs. "Never been very good at it. But sometimes, you have to do things you don't like."

"Like homework?"

"Yeah, like homework." He stood, and Charity hurriedly took a couple steps back so that they wouldn't be right in each other's personal space.

Except she suddenly very much *wanted* to be in his personal space. She wanted for him to hold her hand, and she wanted to bury her nose in the crook of his neck as he embraced her until she had her fill of the warmth from him and that slightly spicy cologne he wore.

"I think this is yours?"

Papa, freed from Savannah's rather wild re-telling, apparently had used that time to find a small wagon not too different from the one they used to harvest from their garden, the bottom of it fairly loaded up with stuff and a painting sticking out of it.

"Oh, thank you!" Alejandro said, striding forward to take the handle of it. "I didn't even think! It would have been a shame to have lost all of this without even getting to taste it."

"I see you have some of Dill and Rebecca's jams in there. Clara and I have been dabbling with that for the past five years, but some of the flavors those two have and the consistency?" Papa Miller shook his head. "We just ain't been able to match it. Good choice there."

Alejandro grinned, looking so very young for a moment. "Really? That's good to hear. I also purchased possibly a year's supply of salsa?"

"If that's Guadalupe's salsa, then no. You bought a couple of months, maybe, depending how good you are at resisting temptation. Those mixes are delicious."

"Good to know I chose well."

"That you did. Maybe tomorrow I can show you all the other best stalls—besides my own, of course—as long as there aren't anymore... interruptions."

He gave Charity a hard look at that, but she just shrugged blithely. Once they were all home, Charlie could give a thorough explanation and she was sure her father would understand why they did what they did.

There was more conversation but then Savannah was yawning, swaying on her feet, and Charity realized just how late it was. Apparently brawling and then dealing with the aftermath really made the time fly. The two made their excuses, and she watched them walk away.

She fully intended to let them do so, but that thread of insecurity pulled through her again and suddenly she was calling after them, jogging forward to catch up. They stopped, to her relief, and she was so caught up in not panting like a lunatic that she didn't really even think about the words coming out of her mouth.

"I'm not always like that, you know. I don't *like* fighting, and I know how to be a lady. But sometimes, you know..." she trailed off, feeling like an utter idiot. "Sometimes you have to rise to the occasion."

Savannah was so tired that she just sort of rubbed her eyes, her brows furrowing, but Alejandro stared at her, dark eyes so intense that he could have been looking right through to her soul.

He wavered, almost like he wasn't sure what he was going to say, but his voice was a deep, low murmur when he did answer. "My wife never backed down from a battle either. Cancer had to fight tooth and nail for everything from her. It's not something you have to apologize for."

Now it was Charity's turn to stare, a rush of emotions filling her. She was... flattered? Also, her heart was pounding. Also, there was a bit of shock too. Of all the things she had expected the man to say or do, *that* wasn't anywhere on the list.

"You have a good night now, Charity."

He tipped his head once more, Savannah waving sleepily, and the two continued down the block. Charity stood there, watching them physically, but her mind was elsewhere, turning his words this way and that.

...because what the heck did *that* mean?

13

Alejandro

"So, what are we doing?"

Alejandro looked up from the book he was reading, the TV playing quietly in the background while Savannah worked on her homework.

"Relaxing?"

She shook her head like he said the silliest things. "No, I mean for your *birthday*. It's your first one in this town and your first one as a doctor with his own practice. It feels, you know, *important*."

"What, like my other birthdays weren't important?"

"No, they were, but I wasn't old enough to tell you how to celebrate them."

"Oh, and you're old enough now?" he teased.

"Well yeah, I've hit the double digits. I'm practically a grown-up."

"Please never say that again."

Her eyes narrowed, and he could see her thoughts cooking behind her eyes. "I won't if you tell me what you want to do for your birthday."

He walked right into that one, didn't he?

It wasn't that Alejandro *hated* his birthday; it was just that it didn't seem like something to celebrate. He remembered vaguely that a coworker had once told him that he seemed checked out, and that was the best explanation he could find for his general apathy about the day.

"Honestly, I would just like to get pizza and relax."

Savannah didn't say anything for a *very* long moment before nodding. "That's boring, but it's your day. If you want pizza and relaxing here, we should do that."

...she gave up much too easily. But maybe that was just the effect Charity was having on her. It had been another two weeks since the festival, and Savannah still went over there each Saturday. Alejandro hadn't stayed, dropping his daughter off, then picking her up later now that he knew he could trust the Millers. And while he enjoyed the time to himself, to catch up on paperwork, bills and emails, he had to admit to himself that he was being a coward.

Because every time he thought of Charity, he thought of how she looked that night, knuckles bloodied and face triumphant, and he'd start to sweat.

It was like he was in high school again, his tongue heavy in his mouth and his heart kicking up impossibly fast. There was something about a strong, daring woman that just *did it* for him, and his mind was playing the whole scene on a loop.

She was wild, a force of nature, all strength and beauty rolled into one package. She was a threat, a warrior, her fierceness written into all her features as she defended both him and her brother.

...he hadn't been so viscerally attracted to a woman in nearly a decade.

Tirza had been so similar. They had met when they were in high school. Some lowlife had snatched her backpack right off of her tiny, freshman frame then booked with it. She'd been chasing the guy down, but her legs were so short that there was no way she was going to catch up to the college-aged man.

Alejandro had been a junior, waiting at the bus stop just like her, and he'd taken after the man without thinking. He caught up and tackled the guy, but once he had him on the ground, he wasn't quite sure what to do from there.

That guy had slugged him, too, and managed to roll over so Alejandro was the one pinned to the ground, and then punched him twice more. Alejandro had known he should let go, but something about that girl's panicked face wouldn't let him.

But it turned out Tirza only needed to catch up with him, because suddenly someone was kicking the man on top of him, knocking him to the side. Before Alejandro could even get up, the tiny little freshman launched herself at the full-grown adult, scratching, biting, and elbowing until he finally managed to wrest her off and split, leaving her backpack on the ground.

That was the moment Alejandro fell in love. But it took Tirza a couple more years to feel the same. He hadn't really minded, of course. Her friendship wasn't a consolation prize. He loved her dearly as a companion and understood when she told him that she wanted to wait until she graduated.

True to her word, she asked him out after she walked

across the stage. That was the happiest day of Alejandro's life up until they married. Then, after that, when Savannah was born.

And Tirza never stopped being a fighter. Even when they found out she was pregnant, despite how careful they were, barely making it from bill to bill with Tirza working two jobs to help put him through school. She was incredibly sick the entire time, and Alejandro begged her to quit her jobs. He would just take a yearlong break from school. He was in his final semester anyway. He was sure they would give him a leave of absence. But she'd told him no. That she believed in him and he was so close. Once he was a doctor, he could baby her and take care of her all he wanted.

Then, when she was diagnosed with cancer, when the chemo made her puke and lose her hair. When the percentages kept getting lower and lower and lower. When Alejandro would wake up with nightmares, so much of him riddled with guilt because *he* was a doctor. He should have been able to help.

Tirza, his beautiful warrior and wife. Her strength had been what had gotten him through all the stress, all the pain.

And then, when he was about to finish his residency and take his final boards, she was gone.

Suddenly Alejandro was a widower, a single father, and then a doctor in a competitive program all at once. Sometimes he was fairly certain the only way he had survived was because he shut himself off; made his body into a machine that could keep running without his soul, without his mind or heart.

For eight long years, the only time he'd really felt truly alive was when he was with Savannah. His beautiful, gifted, amazing daughter who promised that there was still good in the world. His child that sometimes looked so much like his wife that he could cry. She was it, the only thing that reminded him there was more than just *existing*.

Until he saw Charity fight for him and her brother.

He hadn't expected it, and it had hit him like a truck. Completely blindsided, he'd wanted to touch her, to kiss the scrapes on her knuckles in a way that was entirely inappropriate for the sister of his patient. She'd been nothing but polite to him, was amazing with Savannah, and yet he couldn't stop himself from wanting to press his lips against her skin until he could find out if she tasted as good as she smelled, even with someone else's beer spilled on her.

Shameful. To her and to Tirza.

So yeah, maybe he was being a coward, but what else was he supposed to do? Some part of him wanted to move on, to honor Tirza's request that he not sink into himself and disappear into his work. But part of him couldn't. Because if he opened himself up again, if he stopped going through the motions, he'd have to *feel* all that he'd been refusing to feel.

And he didn't know if he'd survive that.

"You have a walk-in, Doc. Are you free?"

Alejandro looked up from the very calendar program he was organizing to see Mrs. Whittaker leaning into his doorway, phone pressed to her ear.

"Actually, I am. What's going on?"

"Miss Sackett says she fell and twisted her ankle."

"She knows we don't do x-rays here, right?"

Mrs. Whittaker nodded. "She says she just needs a pair of

crutches for getting around the house and wants you to take a look at it just to be safe."

"Alright, well, have her come in during one of the spots that canceled."

"Sounds good, Doc."

Alejandro felt the corner of his mouth go up at the term. No one had ever called him Doc back in San Diego, but it seemed a common moniker where he was now.

Time passed quickly and before he knew it, Mrs. Whittaker was knocking on his small office door to tell him that Miss Sackett was in the exam room. He made his way there after a few moments and opened the exam room door to see a young woman there.

She had to be in her twenties, made up and dressed in leggings and a flowing, sheer tunic with an opaque tank underneath. Her lips were a deep plum to match the necklace sitting along her neckline.

Oh.

Alejandro had been a doctor enough to know what different outfits meant when people showed up on a whim. And at the moment, Miss Sackett was wearing a classic "seduce the doctor" look.

He hadn't always recognized it on sight, but a year after he joined his practice, one of his female colleagues had laughed at another disappointed bachelorette slinking out of their building with a flustered sort of air. Once she explained that it wasn't normal for young and middle-aged women to show up to appointments done up like they were going on a date, he couldn't believe he didn't see it before.

Then again, ever since his wife died, he'd forgotten that he could be attractive. He was so much of a shell with a gaping, bleeding wound where his heart was supposed to be, surely everyone around him would be able to tell.

"Hey there, Doc," Miss Sackett said with a sweet grin. "Thank you for fitting me in on such short notice."

She was pretty, that was for certain, but Alejandro wasn't interested. His heart was buried six feet deep with his beloved.

"Of course. I'm sorry you had a tumble. You want to tell me what happened?"

"Well, I was talking to Felita as we were leaving work, and I guess I wasn't watching where I was going because I stepped off the curb wrong and rolled my ankle!"

"And did you hear any clicking noises or pops?"

"No, thank goodness, but when I stood, I couldn't put pressure on it. It's pretty swollen right now."

She pulled the bottom part of her leggings up and, sure enough, her ankle was swollen and red. Oh, so she hadn't been lying about that.

...which meant that she'd really been injured, then drove home, did herself up and changed, then drove back.

Wait, her hair was slightly damp at the top. Had she *showered* while she was in pain with a sprained ankle? Alejandro was *not* worth the effort.

"That does look angry. I'm going to palpate it just to make sure of a few things, is that alright with you?"

The woman blushed, barely visible below her makeup, and he did as he said he would, making sure it really was just a sprain. Once he was sure, he went and got her crutches and walked her through using them. He was about to dismiss her to rest and relax at home with a doctor's note for a few days off work, when suddenly she very obviously tripped, colliding with his chest.

He caught her, because of course he wasn't going to let an

already injured woman slam into the ground, but he quickly righted her and stepped back as she murmured a flushed, flimsy excuse.

"Please be careful, Miss Sackett," he said as professionally as he could.

He could feel the disappointment radiating from the young woman as she nodded then clumsily walked out using her crutches, passing his next patient without even looking up.

"Geez, I thought y'all doctors were supposed to fix people's hearts, not break them."

Surprised, Alejandro looked to the man waiting, trying to remember if he had already met the patient or not. But then he recognized the same cap and square face with red, veining scars up his neck and down his bare arms, raised and an angry red with darker tones below some of the deeper ones.

"Ah, Nathaniel," he said, stepping to the side. "I just have to clean up in here and I'll be right with you."

"It's Nathan, actually. Nathan Westbrook, remember. And I've never met a Doc who actually had to pick up after himself. Aren't you supposed to have a nurse or something for that? The last guy did."

"We're short a medical secretary," Alejandro said with a laugh. "They'll often help since this is such a small practice. But I personally think doctors would benefit from making sure they clean up between patients."

"Ain't that something. Well, do what'cha gotta do."

"That I will."

With a nod, he set about doing exactly that. But as he went through the familiar motions, his mind couldn't help but drift back to Charity. From how Savannah seemed to click with her, to the strange sort of ache he felt whenever he looked at her.

And he really, *really* wanted to look at her again.

14

___

Charity

Charity was trotting along on her horse, enjoying an afternoon walk to declutter her thoughts when her phone rang. Fishing it out of her pocket was surprisingly challenging while sitting on a horse, but she managed in time to see it was Savannah calling her.

Huh, that was weird.

"Is everything okay?"

"Yeah, why wouldn't it be?" Savannah said, her grin evident in her tone.

"Because you're calling me on a school day and not texting. Did you miss your bus again?"

"No. I mean, yes, I'm going to. Look, can you just come pick me up at the Principal's office?"

"Principal's office? If you're in trouble, you should really call your dad."

"No! Don't call my dad!" The urgency of her voice surprised Charity and her horse stopped on instinct, wuffling inquisitively. "Look, I'm not in trouble and nothing is wrong. Just please come pick me up at school, okay?"

"Alright. I'm trusting you. I'll be there in about half an hour; you kind of caught me while I was out riding."

"It would be pretty silly if I was upset at a cowgirl for doing cowboy things. I'll see you then."

Despite Savannah's assurances, Charity was still nervous that something was wrong. Thankfully, good ol' Bernard was a good galloper and took her home fast and true. She was going to need to get him some extra treats as a thank-you, but that would have to wait.

Her palms were sweatier than she would like to admit when she pulled up to where Savannah was waiting. The girl once more launched herself into the truck like a missile and immediately started talking about a mile a minute.

"I want to plan a surprise party for my Dad. It can't be super, super big because he gets overwhelmed easily, but it has to be fun. And not just old people fun, but like, *real* fun. I want him to make friends. If I don't drag him to your ranch, he doesn't go anywhere. And you should have seen him when we were shopping at the festival. He was having so much fun! And it wasn't just because of me!

"So I'd like it if you could order things for me. I have money—I've been saving my allowance ever since we moved here—but if I order them all to the house, Dad'll know. I'm not old enough to have an online account for anything, so I'm only allowed to use his with supervision."

It all mashed together into a sort of word slurry, but Charity was pretty sure she got the gist of it. "Why didn't you just tell me over the phone or text me?"

"Well, one, because I didn't want my dad to see any messages. Two... well..."

It wasn't like Savannah to be reticent. "Come on now. Out with it."

"Well... I might be making these new friends at school myself, but they didn't really believe that I was friends with one of the Millers. Or a cowgirl. When I told them you were one and the same, they told me I was full of it."

Charity looked past the girl, out her open truck window to see there were indeed several other children watching her pick Savannah up. Unlike Savannah, those kids actually looked their age, and it was almost adorable how they strained to see who it was in the truck. If she'd had a child when she'd first started trying... they'd be just older than Savannah, right?

But that had never worked out, had it...

Shaking her head, she gave the kids a wave before driving off a bit faster than was strictly necessary. Savannah let out a squeal of delight, and Charity was sure that the young girl wouldn't have any more problems being believed.

They arrived at Savannah's house rather quickly and Savannah happily talked the entire ten minutes about her grand ideas. She was a sweet girl, she really was, and her love for her father was so apparent.

"Alright, just text me a list and I'll get you whatever you need to make this thing happen."

"Really?" Savannah half-shrieked, half-squealed. Goodness, children could really hit an octave all of their own, couldn't they?

"Yeah, why not? Besides, you and your dad deserve a nice party."

"Thank you, thank you!" And then the girl was looking at

her with such serious eyes that Charity was almost taken aback. "I think you're the best thing that's happened to us in years."

Charity stared for a moment, lost for words, but Savannah just lunged across the seats to press a quick kiss to her cheek then bolted out of the car. By the time Charity came back to herself, the young girl was already halfway up her porch steps.

"Bye! See you this Saturday!"

"See you!" Charity managed to call back, waiting until the girl was inside before pulling away. But her cheek tingled slightly, and her heart got achy just like it did every time she thought about her non-existent children and all the things they'd never gotten to do.

So many cheek kisses, so many hugs, so many birthdays that just never were. And simply because her body just didn't want to cooperate with her. It seemed cruel that someone who wanted children so desperately had been denied.

Ugh, why was she thinking such depressing things when she had a precocious young girl to help with a great party?

She managed to make it home without slipping into her melancholy and went up to her room. She didn't spend a ton of time there, preferring to be out and about and doing things. Her Papa was much the same, which was why he'd chosen to settle someplace so warm. She definitely appreciated his foresight.

Sure enough, as soon as she got herself a drink and settled down with her laptop, her phone buzzed with several texts in quick succession. Was... was Savannah texting each item individually?

Opening her phone, she saw no, the young girl wasn't. But she did have breaks every so often when she needed to give an exact brand of something, or lengthy reason as to why she was asking for it.

It was easy enough to do, the list being clear and concise, and Charity had to chuckle a couple of times at the earnestness of the child. She really was planning on a heck of a shindig, and the thoughtfulness was touching.

But perhaps the task was a little *too* simple, because her mind began to wander again, drifting to what she could have been doing if she and her ex had worked out. Secretly planning surprise parties and scheming in the best of ways. Eric would expect that something was up, of course, he had a mind for plotting, but he would still act completely blindsided when he walked into the door to their—two? three? five?—children all waiting for him in the dark.

"Get it together, Charity," she hissed to herself, finishing up the list. It wasn't good to linger in the past or dream about a perfect world. The truth was that she didn't have kids, she couldn't ever have kids, and her husband had found comfort in the arms of another woman because of it, then tried to extort her family for money with a long and vicious divorce.

It was a good thing that they had never had kids, because Charity knew without a doubt that he would have used them as pawns and put them in the middle. But still... it was a life she had dreamed of for so long, and sometimes she longed for the innocence of it.

Sometimes, it felt like no one else in her family understood. She was the first divorce in three generations, and while her family supported her, none of them *understood*.

Well, Papa understood what it was like to lose his beloved, and he hadn't dated a single soul since. And Alejandro did too...

No wonder he seemed to be just as much of a lonely soul as she was.

15

———

Alejandro

Alejandro was tired.

Not just worn out, not just sleepy, but bones-deep, utterly ragged sort of exhausted.

He was just slipping into his car after finishing a *very* long, gray day of work after a very, very long week of work. His schedule had been full from open to close with appointments as well as interviews, Mrs. Whittaker happy in her position but reminding him that they needed to find *someone* before the holidays set in.

It wasn't that Alejandro didn't like the ten women who had come in to interview so far, but Mrs. Whittaker politely advised him that they wouldn't be a good match for their little dynamic, and he tended to listen to her.

Of course, he asked her why at first, making sure it wasn't just personal bias, but she always had good reasons. Miss

Sackett showed up, limping slightly, and Mrs. Whittaker confirmed that the young woman was looking more for a wedding ring than a job, and her niece had overheard the girl talking about how she was aiming to get her Mrs. degree courtesy of Alejandro.

So naturally, she was no longer a candidate.

After that there was a young man named James who seemed promising, but then Mrs. Whittaker said that his mother said he had been accepted to his dream college, so he would only be around for about six months. They should be looking to train someone more long term.

Then there was Isabella, but it turned out that she was just on an LOA from college after taking time off for reasons Mrs. Whittaker didn't share, but she was going back after the winter break.

Then there was Melissa, who was a notorious gossip who always tried to start drama at her last previous workplaces, Jamie, who was a school bully who terrorized most of Mrs. Whittaker's nieces and nephews, and Julio, who would have been an excellent addition, but as Alejandro was preparing to call the young man back and offer him the position, he received an email that Julio had just been hired by his first choice practice the next town over and would be moving.

There were more, but they all began to blend together. Alejandro just wanted to find *someone,* but he recognized that he needed someone who would fit. Especially since they were a skeleton crew in a tiny town. Back in San Diego, there had been two nightmare medical secretaries who made life so much worse than it ever had to be.

Oh well. It would have to wait another week. Because it was finally Friday, and Saturday was his birthday with pizza and Savannah and tons of relaxation.

He made his way back home, thinking only of his bed, and his body felt so *heavy* by the time he finally thunked up the porch. The lights were off, so he assumed that Savannah was probably already asleep or taking a long bath.

That turned out to be a very wrong assumption, however, because as soon as he turned the entryway light on, suddenly people were jumping out at him and yelling *surprise!*

Alejandro stood there a moment, shocked and only able to stare at all the people crammed into his house that was now decorated for a party.

There were blue and gold streamers, one of his favorite color combinations, as well as some balloons. Shiny, metallic swirls hung from the ceiling, with a few cheery centerpieces on the coffee table, kitchen counters, and who knew where else.

"What..." was all he managed to say for a second.

But then Savannah was bounding up and launched herself at him. *Omph!* Soon, she wouldn't be able to do that. "Happy Birthday, Dad! I got you pizza!"

"And a lot more, it would seem."

Finally, his brain seemed to catch up with what was happening, and he recognized the faces around him. There was Mrs. Whittaker, who had made an excuse earlier to leave early that suddenly made a whole lot more sense. There was Papa Miller, Charity and her brother, Charlie, but Clara and Cass were missing. There was his uncle-in-law Jacob, white-haired and freckled through his tan, and his aunt-in-law, Juanita. So, not a *huge* crowd, but definitely everyone that he was even relatively close with.

His eyes flashed back to catch another glimpse of Charity. It was the closest he'd been to her since that night at the festival.

"I hope you like it," Savannah said into his chest as she hugged him. "I know you said just pizza and relaxing, but you deserve something special." She looked up at him, her eyes so big and full of hope. "I got you ice cream cake and other stuff too!"

How could he resist a face like that? Besides, he liked every person who was present. "Thank you, Savannah. This is great."

"Yay! Here, let me show you everything!"

She took his hand and did indeed show him *everything*. Her decorations, a pile of presents that seemed more akin to a kid's party than a grown man's. And more impressively, the *spread*.

Although Clara wasn't present, it was clear that she'd at least had some hand in the food on the table. There were wings and plenty of tortilla chips, but there was also fried chicken and some sort of roasted mini sausage on toothpicks. And then he spotted Juanita's legendary tamales and he *knew* it was going to be a good party.

Maybe it was telling that the very first thing he did was fill his plate and then grab a cold beer that some amazing soul brought in, but Savannah had gotten her good eating gene from *someone,* and it wasn't her mother. He was just about to sit himself down on the sofa and try some friendly, grown-up conversation when suddenly Charity was beside him.

Goodness, she certainly moved quietly when she wasn't in her cowboy boots. "I know we're supposed to be nice to you as the birthday boy, but you look dead tired."

"That's because I am," Alejandro said with a chuckle. "Before you guys all gave me a heart attack, I was thinking about refamiliarizing myself with my bed and eight hours of uninterrupted sleep."

"Wow, you're a wild man."

"Wouldn't be the first time I was called that," he said without thinking, sending her a grin.

And of course, her eyebrows shot straight up. "Oh really? Is that so?"

"Hey there, Alejandro! For moving to my neck of the woods, we sure don't see each other much."

And it was his uncle-in-law who saved the day, coming in and wrapping Alejandro in a hug. He let himself be led away and pulled into a conversation, wondering what it was about Charity that made him say the lamest things.

Despite how exhausted he'd been, the conversation and the food perked him up, and he found himself having fun. There was quiet music playing in the background, he was surrounded by nice people that he trusted, and his stomach was full.

Savannah, of course, was having the time of her life. She had set out Uno as well as playing cards, and always had at least someone to play with her until, at about eight o'clock, she announced that she was going to bed.

It was early for her, considering her bedtime had been nine p.m. since she turned ten and she didn't have to be up until seven, *and* it was the weekend, but then she bounded over to kiss him on the cheek and tell him to have fun for at least a little longer before kicking everyone out.

He got it then. His little girl was giving him time where he not only didn't have to watch or worry about her, but also so that he couldn't use her as a crutch. She was so smart, that one. Far too smart. And he loved it so, *so* much.

But then she kept on talking.

"Now you don't have to worry about me hogging Charity so much."

"What was that now?"

"Goodnight! See you in the morning!"

She skipped off, the little miscreant, and Alejandro's gaze automatically shifted to find the woman in question.

She was standing in the kitchen, leaning against the counter as she drained a beer and her brother voraciously helped himself to some of everything. The young man had eaten plenty the two times Alejandro had stayed for a meal, but *wow*, the guy could really put it away.

But even the impressive amount of food the second youngest Miller child ate couldn't distract him from Charity more than a couple of moments. She was wearing leggings with a galaxy pattern on them and a simple, oversized slouchy hoody that went down to her mid-thigh. It was so different from both her working clothes that he usually saw her in and her corn festival clothes, but drew him in just the same, his eyes sliding along the length of her.

And perhaps most noticeably of all, her hair was down. Sure, she had a couple braids near her temples that were pulled back into a colorful hair tie at the back of her head, but other than that the long, long auburn waves tumbled in gentle waves down her back, all the way just past her butt.

Alejandro's fingers itched with the desire to run themselves through her hair, to feel how soft and silky it was. He wanted to bury his hand in it while she hugged him, encouraging her to tilt her head upwards so he could kiss those perfect li—

"You look like you're thinking about something."

Alejandro shot back into his body at the sound of Papa Miller's voice and looked guiltily to the patriarch. Oh, that was awkward. The older man just caught him ogling his daughter right in front of him.

Uh…

"No. Nothing."

"Aw, is that so? And here I hoped maybe you were thinking about Charity."

Alejandro practically choked on his beer, swallowing hard and coughing. "Come again?"

"I love my girl, I do, but the truth is she's gone through some things that have hurt her. Real bad. She tries to hide it, pretend that she's alright, but a father knows, you know?"

"Uh-huh," Alejandro said, taking another long drink. Because what else was he supposed to say?

"But when she's around you and your little girl, she lights up. She laughs and smiles, even if she's not taking care of someone. It's nice to see my girl back." Papa Miller sighed and sat down next to Alejandro. Which was weird. The whole situation was weird. "Pardon an old man for meddling, I just can't help but think… well, that you two have some things in common that most people don't."

"Do we?" Alejandro asked. He couldn't help it. His eyes went right back to Charity, who was laughing and shoving a chicken wing into Charlie's mouth.

"I don't know your exact story, but it's clear you lost someone. And Charity just about had her heart ripped out and stomped on. At first I thought maybe you were just enjoying someone taking your girl off your hands for a quick rest, but then I saw how you looked at Charity at the corn festival and I started to get an inkling maybe it wasn't just the free babysitting."

It was all so *much*. Yeah, Alejandro could feel himself being pulled towards the woman. He found himself looking to her hands, remembering what it felt like to hold them in his, thinking about all the incredible things that she could make.

He looked to her face, with those intense eyes and her plush lips, the clever words that would tumble out of them.

But he still felt that same anchor in him, the one that tethered him to Tirza and the future they were supposed to have together but never was. Stepping away from that felt like a betrayal. He already had his perfect life. His happily ever after. And yeah, it was gone along with Tirza, but that didn't mean he got to have another.

He'd never wanted to let go of the anchor before either. He was content to let it drag him into the deepest depths, to sink him into the dark until he didn't have to think or feel anymore.

...why was it when he looked at Charity, he almost wanted to *try?*

"Again, hope I wasn't butting in, but you seem like a decent man and I just wanted to let you know—in case you were stuck in your own head—that you aren't imagining the chemistry between you two. Cass has been going on about it since the second time she met you, although she'd probably kill me for mentioning that."

"She what?"

Wait... she'd been the one who invited Savannah over, right? And during her appointments, she sure did manage to drop a lot of information about her family that mostly concerned Charity.

Huh.

That was something to think about.

"Ah, I've said too much. If you don't mind me, I'm going to go pretend I didn't meddle."

Papa Miller stood, giving Alejandro a tip of his beer bottle and then he was wandering over to the card games where an older woman was playing with Mrs. Whittaker.

Alejandro hadn't spotted her before, but if he remembered right, that was the school librarian that he'd only met once but that Savannah talked about almost as much as she talked about Charity.

He didn't know how he'd missed her earlier, but then again, the shock at the door had been pretty intense. He was surprised he even remembered English after that jolt to the brain and heart.

...he was distracting himself, wasn't he?

Yeah, he was. And just like all the other times, his attention went back to Charity.

Except she wasn't in the kitchen anymore, just her brother, who was dumping a truly impressive pile of eaten wings into the trash. Thankfully whoever had brought the two giant platters had sprung for a *lot*, because there was still plenty left.

Taking another swallow of his beer, Alejandro stood and walked to the kitchen, lingering in the doorway to see if he could catch a glimpse of the woman in question.

"If you're looking for Charity, she went on the porch for a breath of fresh air. Parties aren't really her thing," Charlie said.

"Am I that obvious?" Alejandro asked, wincing.

He was a widower, that was his identity. He was used to people not believing it, and people saying he should move on, but what he wasn't used to was everyone seeming to think that he already was pining for someone.

Because he wasn't. ...was he?

Sure, he felt a strange, alien pull in his chest towards Charity. Looking at her made him remember what it used to be like to feel desire. To crave physical touch and comfort. To come home to a partner and have someone to rely on.

But he was probably just lonely. Tired. He'd moved to a new town and took over a whole practice entirely on his own.

That was stressful. He wasn't betraying Tirza's memory and he didn't have chemistry with the capable eldest daughter of a millionaire family.

And yet he was walking towards the porch, stepping out of his front door, and letting it close quietly behind him.

"Hey there," he said, interrupting the reverie Charity seemed to be in, her face tipped up towards the stars, reflecting the light almost blue on her skin. He almost felt guilty, disrupting her peace like that, but he also felt selfish, like he wanted to talk to her forever and take up all of her time until she was sick of him.

Strange. Very strange. Drawn to her like a moth to light but repelled by the idea of letting go of his anchor.

"Hey," she said back, her expression more melancholy than anything else. She looked so *hurt*, and he couldn't understand why. She'd seemed so happy a few minutes ago.

"Party get too overwhelming for you?"

"Something like that."

"May I join you?"

She nodded from where she was leaning against the banister, on the small corner of the porch that wasn't covered by the awning. Cautiously, he walked over to her, almost as if he was worried any sudden movement would startle her and she'd disappear in a cloud of smoke.

So then, a few moments later, they were both leaning against the banister, looking up at the night sky.

It really was beautiful. He felt like a cliché, but in San Diego, the night sky hadn't been anything like it was in the country. Bright points of light shimmering in the plush cobalt of the night sky, winking and glistening like so many possible wishes in the quiet of the night.

And there were no words. Maybe he should have said

something, anything, but nothing came. He was too rusty, too sunk into the depth of the nothing he'd let himself fall into.

Finally, it was Charity who broke the silence, because of course it had to be her.

"Savannah told me about her mother."

"Ah." He had figured as much. He liked to think he could be everything and all the things for Savannah, but the truth is she was a growing young woman and had questions that she probably only felt comfortable asking from another woman. "And...?"

"There's no 'and.' Just that I know... Just that I know and I'm sorry."

"What do you have to be sorry about?"

Charity didn't say anything for a moment, and he could feel her posture stiffening, and finally she turned to him. "I'm sorry because lately, when I think about it, I feel happy that there's someone out there besides my own father who understands what it's like."

"What... what's like?"

"Having half of your heart ripped out when you were so sure that you'd have it forever."

Oh.

...oh.

Her father said that she'd been hurt, and there she was on his porch, talking about how she understood his heartbreak. Maybe... maybe they were even more alike than he thought.

He remembered Tirza holding his hand, making him promise to grieve and move on, telling him that he couldn't wrap his identity around being a widower. That he had to push himself, had to make his world bigger than just his daughter.

He hadn't done that. Not even remotely. He had never

cared to. But maybe... maybe he owed it to Tirza. He owed it to Savannah.

And maybe he owed it to himself.

"I... didn't know that you'd lost someone too."

"Not in the same way. I think yours is worse. But still, it's nice to see that it's possible to live, maybe even flourish after something like that."

She thought he was *living*? *Flourishing*?

He was empty most of the time, except when he was in the presence of his daughter. He went to work. He came home. The most socializing he'd done in nearly a decade was the party behind him.

"I'm... I'm not, I..."

"Sorry, sorry. It's your birthday and here I am pushing all my baggage onto you. Go in, enjoy yourself."

"I don't mind. It's kind of a lot for me too. And I like being out here talking with you."

She looked over to him and goodness, the smile on her face. It was so soft, so sweet. He couldn't help his own grin from matching hers, and he wanted to memorize the moment forever.

How had he never noticed that her eyes were so green, with deep honeyed flecks centered around her iris then spattering outward like a gem. He could see those same, glittering stars in them, impossibly beautiful against their shining background.

"That's good then." She flushed and took a deep breath, and then normal, headstrong Charity was back. "We should probably get inside."

She started to move away from him, started to break the moment, and he just felt so *selfish* that he didn't want it to end.

The next thing he knew, words were coming out of his mouth in a jumbled rush.

"We could go out sometime, if you wanted."

It was so fast that even he couldn't quite understand the hurried mash of syllables.

"Huh?" Charity answered. "You said you wanna stay outside?"

No, that's not what he said at all. But the moment *was* gone, and suddenly all that courage that pushed the words out were gone and he was falling back into the dark, clinging to his anchor and letting it hold him in the deep waters where he didn't have to feel anything.

"Yeah, I would like to stay outside a few more minutes."

"Okay, you do that. I'll see you around, Alejandro. And happy birthday, again, in case I don't get a chance to say it later."

"Thank you, Charity. Really."

"Of course, what else are friends for?"

16

———

Alejandro

"**W**hat on earth is *wrong* with you?"

Alejandro pulled himself out of his mind, blinking at Cass Miller. He was in the middle of going through one of her checkups and everything had been going normally, so he wasn't sure why she was suddenly biting at him.

"Pardon?"

"I thought you had a thing for Charity, and you had a prime opportunity to ask her out at your birthday, Charlie even told you where she was on the porch, but you just… didn't? Like, what's with that?"

Oh, it was about *that*?

It had been four days since his birthday and every time he slowed down, he thought of how he bungled it with Charity. He also thought about fixing it, about texting her, calling her, *anything*. But he didn't.

The words wouldn't come out.

So he went through the motions like usual, only for Cass to verbally snap him out of it.

"I like your sister just fine, but—"

"Don't 'but' me. I've never seen someone who makes moony eyes at her with nearly the regularity that you do. Sometimes I'm worried that your heart is going to flop right out of your chest onto our kitchen table."

She leaned forward, her features all standing out in sharp relief against her increasingly pale skin. Was she spending enough time outside? Getting sun and vitamin D exposure? Probably not.

"Look, if you don't want to, or weren't interested, it'd be one thing. But you stare at her like you're a terribly lovesick puppy, and you *followed* her onto the porch when there was no reason to. So, I'm asking, one adult to the other, what gives?"

"Nothing gives. Nothing is wrong. I just..." What could he say? That he felt attracted to Charity, yes. That he liked talking to her? Sure. That he was too scared to give anything a chance because that would mean letting go of his anchor. His grief. His guilt. Those were familiar to him, comforting in their own way.

"Savannah is still getting over the loss of her mother. It wouldn't be fair to her to—"

"Bull."

Alejandro jolted at her firm but flat rebuttal, cutting away the excuse he was so used to using on himself and any coworkers who became too opinionated. "Pardon?"

"Did you forget that my mom died too? That I had to watch, as a kid, bit by bit while she just... unraveled? Rotted?"

Oh, he had forgotten. For just a few moments. Was that

the loss that Papa Miller had been talking about? Charity was the eldest; perhaps she was the one who remembered her mother the most.

"Not to be blunt, but Savannah was just over two when her mom passed. She wasn't really old enough to understand that her mother was sick, or even that she was dead. Growing up, she's had to learn what that means, but all of her world is based around you."

Alejandro felt a flare of defensiveness and crossed his arms. "Oh, and you're an expert on my daughter?"

"No, but I'm her friend, and I *am* an expert on watching my mother die. I'm an expert on growing up with a father who was grieving so terribly but trying to force himself to be strong. And you know what, he *still* hasn't moved on. It's been over a decade, and my dad is *so* lonely. All he has is us and his garden and the ranch. That's it. No real friends, just friendly acquaintances. No dating. Nothing.

"And it *hurts.* I want Papa to be happy. I want him happy and healthy and with an equal partner who he can share things with, grow with, find solace in."

She sat up straighter, her finger poking into his chest like a firebrand.

Cass continued, "You don't think Savannah feels the same way? She's the smartest little girl I've ever met, and even if she doesn't always understand emotions, she still *feels* them. You think that she doesn't want her daddy to not be so *sad* all the time? Look, the pain of her loss will always be there, but if it's not addressed, it just grows and grows and festers."

"...I'm not sad all the time."

"Aren't you? Look me in my eyes and tell me you're fine with your life, that you have no interest in my sister, and I'll never say a thing again. And if you want, I'll even find a doctor in the city to take care of me, so you never have to deal with any of us again."

The thought of his ties to the Millers being yanked away made his heart stutter. No Cass appointments meant not seeing Charity during the week. And if he banished her from his practice, Savannah probably wouldn't be able to visit the ranch on the weekend and she would be *so* disappointed.

"*No*," he said, much more emphatically than he meant to. "...no. I don't want you all gone."

"Awfully telling, that was. Look, just give me *one* good reason for you not to try at least. And that reason can be as small as you just don't want to, because I can get that. What I can't get is you stopping yourself from doing what you *really* want to do... just to punish yourself."

"It's *not* just to punish myself!"

He was startled by the emphasis he managed to put into that sentence without shouting, but there was steel to his words.

"Then what is it?"

"I... I don't know if I can put it into words. The best I can try to explain it is... I've been living in a world where there's no color. At first it was awful; everything I saw was so *wrong*. But as time went on, the lack of color became less jarring. Then it became normal. And now I'm so used to living in this black-and-white world that it's all I know."

He swallowed, his words slowing as his brain caught up. He was really telling his personal life to his patient, which was probably a huge violation of ethics, but he was just so *tired* of the whirlwind of spinning thoughts in his head.

"And now, when I'm around Charity, when I look at Charity, some of the color bleeds through. It's just little tendrils now, and they're so... so *much* after so long that they're just as terrifying as they are captivating."

She stared at him for a very long time, and he could see her thoughts flashing behind her eyes, but he had no idea what they were. Eventually, however, she sat back and let out a long breath.

"I get that. I do. Thanks, for trusting me with that. Sorry I kind of blew up at you. Since the accident, sometimes I get, uh, aggressive, I guess."

"That's normal for a type A like yourself."

"Type A? Are you calling me an—"

"No! *No.* Type A just means very determined and driven, sometimes to your own detriment. Type A's can push themselves too far and not listen to their body, or, if their ability to accomplish their goals is compromised, can turn self-destructive if they don't have an outlet for their energy."

"Ah. Right. Well, I suppose that makes sense. Although maybe that first one did too... wait. You're distracting me. You stop that."

Alejandro breathed out a short sigh. He had thought that, for a moment, he'd managed to move on from the topic. "Can't blame me for trying."

"No, I suppose I can't, Mr. Black-and-White. I can't force you to do anything, but I will warn you, if you start to play a will-they-won't-they game with my sister after everything she's been through, we'll see just how type A I can go on your kneecaps."

Perhaps if it was someone else, Alejandro would have been irritated, maybe even felt threatened. But there was just enough of a hint of hurt below her words that it worked.

Losing their mother had wounded all of the Miller siblings in an intense way, and it made sense how much they wanted to protect each other. Maybe if Savannah had a sibling of her own...

"Understood. I guess I have a lot to think about."

"You certainly do."

17

Charity

"So, to seal this off without making the vacuum suction too strong to be easily opened..."

Charity paused the video and scribbled into her draft book, chewing on the end of her pencil hard enough to get eraser bits in her mouth. Starting, she lurched forward and spat them out, disturbing sweet little Fern from where she'd been casually munching on some grass.

"Sorry, sorry," she said, wiping her mouth and sitting up. She was behind the work shack, taking a break while trying to plot out some new ways to make the house more accessible for Cass.

One thing she noticed was how sore her sister got on the days she returned from her appointments with Alejandro or when she pushed herself especially hard. And Cass had always been a huge fan of baths, with her own collection of salts and special oils in the bathroom that she and Charity shared between their rooms. They had a lovely, whirlpool tub that was plenty deep, but twice now Cass had been in there for hours, stuck in the slick tub long after it drained. Charity was so irritated that her younger sister wouldn't let her help Cass out of the tub, but she couldn't exactly argue with wanting to maintain at least some dignity.

So, her idea was to somehow make it easier to get in and out of, but it wasn't even a standard tub, so there was a lot to meddle with. And she could just rip out the tub and put in a newer one that was more accessible, but they would lose all the jets that Cass loved so much.

"Come on, Charity. Just think."

But her thoughts were so messy and churning, rotating over and over again until they went right back to the party.

She hadn't meant for anything to happen at the party, and technically nothing *did* happen, but for a moment it almost seemed like it *would*.

Charity had been on the porch, trying to get some air. She thought she could handle being in close proximity to Alejandro in his own house, but it had all been too much. Being in his home, seeing the pictures of him and Savannah through different stages of her life. Seeing him smile, seeming to enjoy himself as he stuffed his face full of delicious food.

And then, while wandering, she saw the wedding pictures and maternity pictures of his late wife.

She had been *so* beautiful, and the way he looked at her, well... it was powerful. There was so much love there, between the two of them, and they looked *so* happy. There was a box in the Miller basement, shoved into the farthest corner, full of happy pictures of Charity's own wedding, but it wasn't the same.

Probably because the woman in the pictures loved Alejandro with all her heart, while Eric had cheated on her then tried to extort her family for money.

It had all been overwhelming at the moment, her inadequacy shoved into her face again, so she'd gone outside. But then Alejandro had come out while she was standing there, and they were so *close*, and the way he was looking at her was so similar to how she *wished* he'd look at her, and the stars were sparkling, and... and...

And then nothing had happened.

She felt ridiculous again, caught up in her own melodrama. He was a grown man, and she was acting like some sort of high school drama character. But no matter how many times she told herself that, her mind just went back to the porch.

Fern made a concerned sound then mouthed at her hair, pulling at the braid. She was a tiny thing, compared to a couple of their horses, but she was loving and sweet—if not sometimes too curious for her own good.

"Hey, okay, girl. We'll go for a ride in a few minutes, okay? You just keep on grazing for now. There are some dandelions over there you missed."

She made an unimpressed sound but let go of Charity's hair and moseyed over to the patch, tail swishing.

"Am I interrupting anything?"

Charity yelped, throwing her pencil as she scrambled up on her feet. "Alejandro!?" she blurted, surprised to see the doctor standing there, dressed up like a dream in a casual gray sweater and jeans with a light jacket. "What are you doing here? You scared the ever-loving potatoes out of me!"

"Sorry about that. I didn't want to interrupt you, but I also didn't want to chicken out."

Didn't want to... what?

"Hey, can we talk for a moment?"

Charity wiped her palms on her pants, feeling nerves bubbling in her stomach. "Uh, sure. Yeah, we can talk." She wanted to crack a joke, but his tone was so serious that she couldn't help but fear the worst. Was he going to tell her that Savannah wasn't allowed over anymore? That she needed smarter, better role models? Or even worse, that her feelings made him uncomfortable and he didn't want to see her ever again.

"Look, I understand that this should probably be easier for a grown man, but I... I haven't even been human for a long time, really."

Hadn't been human? What? Charity felt she was a few steps behind.

"If you're about to tell me you're a werewolf, I think you're in the wrong genre. Ain't never heard of a cowboy lycanthrope," she said.

He laughed at that, and she relaxed ever so slightly. He probably wouldn't laugh if he was about to ban her from his life completely.

"Lycanthrope? That sounds like a word of the day."

"Only in a very specific calendar for very specific people."

"Right." The light laughter faded and then it was just her and him, standing behind her workshop, two awkward adults and the need to "talk" apparently. "Look, I... I'm not very good at this. But uh, I was hoping..." He took a deep breath.

What was he trying to say? He wasn't good at *what*? Setting boundaries? Letting people down?

He continued, "I... would..." Another deep breath. "Do you want to go grab dinner sometime?"

Wait.

Wait a little more.

Was he *asking her out*?

That was impossible. He was a dashing doctor with caramel skin and salt and pepper just at the temples of his thick, black hair. He was all dashing good looks and brilliant smarts, and she was an infertile divorcée who just puttered around her father's ranch.

She didn't say anything, staring at the four heads that he definitely just grew all at once, trying to figure out what other way he could have meant it. Because he had to have meant it another way... right?

Alejandro let out the slightest chuckle. "You're making me nervous," he said.

She could tell he was aiming for levity, but that quickly fell away when she just kept staring at him. Where were her *words*? She needed words and they just wouldn't come out.

He shuffled his feet. "I'm sorry if I crossed a line. I just—"

"Why on earth would you want to do something like that?"

There it was: a slight flush on his cheeks and a look of utter heartbreak settling on his face. "Right, of course. I apologize. I never should have, I shouldn't—"

No! She was ruining it. She was ruining it and she didn't even mean to. But part of her mind was stuck on the fact that it *had* to be a prank. Or a joke. Or a misunderstanding. Sure, she'd hoped that maybe there might be *something* between them. But that would be ridiculous.

Except...

Except he was standing in front of her, looking embarrassed and crushed, and he—oh! He was turning away from her to go! She had to stop him.

"Wait!" Before her mind could catch up, she was lunging forward to grab his wrist. He turned back to her, and the movement brought them so close to each other. The closest they'd ever been physically, with not even an arm's length between them. "I'm sorry. Don't go. I'm just... I need to clarify. Are you asking me out?"

The look he gave her was full of so much weight. "I realize I don't always give the clearest of signals, but yeah. I would like to take you to dinner. And I'm terrified of that, Charity. I haven't done anything like this in years."

She let out a laugh that was entirely shaky. "No one has asked me out since I was seventeen."

His eyebrows furrowed and now it was his turn to look at her like she'd grown some extra heads herself. "How is that possible?"

Ugh. So much baggage. It was all strapped to her back, slowing her down, and she knew that she should tell him so he would realize that she was damaged goods and go about his merry way, but the words were thick and heavy on her tongue.

Surely it wouldn't be too wrong of a thing to enjoy *one* date? To let herself revel in being seen as a woman, as desirable.

No, it was selfish. But maybe... maybe Charity was ready to be a little selfish.

"Long story. But yes. I would very much like to grab dinner. With you. I, uh... when?"

"How about next Friday? I can pick you up and we can go to uh, whichever restaurant you like more?"

"Uh, I like authentic Mexican food so we can go to *El Huerto Secreto,* if you want?"

"Are you just saying that because I'm Latino?"

"What! No!" Alarm rose in her before she saw the cheeky grin on Alejandro's face, and she let out a frustrated sound.

"You jerk!" she accused, letting go of his wrist to playfully bat at his arm.

"I have been known to dabble in jerkdom from time to time. I'll see you on Friday after six?"

"Okay. Just remember that it's been a long time since I've been on a date. I'm probably rusty."

"Don't worry, I am too."

18

———————

Charity

How was it Friday already!?

Charity paced in her room, back and forth, back and forth. Her hair was still dripping from her shower, but she couldn't quite bring herself to look in her closet and pick something out. Because doing that made it too real.

And while she was excited about the date, that she was going to have a chance to get closer to Alejandro, she also knew that she would inevitably mess it up. Because that's what she did. No one wanted a brawling, barren, divorcée thirty-two-year-old girlfriend and especially not a handsome, successful doctor who had his own practice.

A knock sounded at Charity's door, bringing her out of her frenzied thoughts.

"Yeah?"

"It's Clara. Do you want some help?"

Charity opened her mouth to say no, because of course she didn't need any help. She was a grown woman. But then she thought better of it. Although Clara was more retro and rockabilly than Charity had any desire to be, there was no denying that she was fashionable. She even made her own clothes.

"Uh yeah. The door is unlocked."

Clara entered and if someone didn't know her, they might not have noticed how excited she was. But her eyes were sparkling, and her lips were pulled up in a mild grin. "Okay, are you feeling a dress, or do you want your legs covered? The forecast tonight is mild and not very breezy, but there's a slight chance of rain after nine."

"You... you know all that?"

"Of course. An important part of planning any look is making sure the environment suits it. You can wear a little number, but if you have to cover it up with a parka, what's the point? If you're gonna go out dancing, you need to make sure you're not going to flash everyone—unless that's your goal, of course."

Charity let out a snort, flopping back onto her bed. "No, I'm not planning on dancing or flashing, not to worry."

"I wasn't. But anyway, dress or bottoms?"

"Dress, I guess. Do I even have any good dresses?"

"Yes, you do."

"How? I haven't bought a dress since..."

Since her first-year anniversary with Eric. Another lifetime ago. He'd always complained that she wasn't feminine enough with her work overalls and tendency to come home covered in either dirt or oil, so she'd stopped buying dresses as a sort of rebellion, she supposed.

A lot of good that had done her.

"Naturally you never noticed, but when was the last time you checked your walk-in closet as opposed to living out of your dresser?"

"Huh?" Charity looked over her shoulder to the closed door in the corner of her room. "Uh, I dunno. Maybe... Ben's wedding? No, Benji's. But those dresses are too formal for—"

"Follow me."

Getting up off her bed, she did as her sister asked, opening the door and stepping in. She rarely used the walk-in, as it was full of special occasion clothes as well as stuff she had outgrown but never thrown away. How could she get rid of her jeans from third grade when those were the jeans her mom had patched so she could keep wearing them? How could she throw away the hoody that her mom had accidentally spilled coffee down when Charity jumped out from behind a corner to startle her during Halloween?

"Here, this section is all the things I've made for you."

Following the direction of her hand, Charity did indeed see that there was a section of the built-in's hanging rod that had several clothing items of different vibrant colors.

"Wait... you've been making things for me?"

"I make things for all of you. What else do you think I do all winter? Not like there's anything to garden, preserve or can."

"I... why didn't you tell me?"

She shrugged. "I figured I would once it was needed, and now it seems like it is. Don't worry, Charlie hasn't found his custom suit jackets I've been making him either."

"Oh...uh, alright. You realize that's a little strange, right?"

"No stranger than most of our family's lives."

"Okay, fair enough. What color should I pick?"

Clara looked over the selections, tapping her chin. Charity

watched her closely instead of the clothes, her chest filling with warmth. She hadn't even known it, but her baby sister had been taking care of her just as much as Charity had been taking care of her sister. They all picked up the slack in different ways after losing Mama; it would do Charity well to remember that and thank her siblings accordingly.

"I think the green would be best. It brings out the red tones in your hair and matches your eyes. And I know you have a pair of nude wedges from the wedding. How about those with it?"

"Okay, yeah. Yeah, that sounds like a plan."

"I know you're not much of a makeup girl, but I have the perfect shade of lipstick."

Clara disappeared, leaving Charity to stare at the dress she'd laid on the bed. It was fitted at the top but filled out into a generous sort of A-line. A petticoat would really make it pop if she wanted to go for an actual retro look, but without one it was passably modern—especially with the boat neck and the capped sleeves.

She could do this. She *could.*

While Clara was gone, she forced herself to get out her appropriate underthings and put them on along with an old, loose T-shirt she could get ready in without worrying about ruining her dress. Her hair came first, and she went to her shared bathroom to dry it out as best she could. She never should have washed it, but once she'd gotten into the shower, she'd been so deep in thought that she hadn't noticed she'd put shampoo in her hair until it was too late.

It was never going to get fully dry in time—it usually took around a day as it were—so she just tried to get it manageable until it was able to be braided, and she worked it up into two loose pigtails atop her head before fish-tail braiding either of those and twisting them in different directions around each other until it looked like she had a fairly complicated and fancy up-do. Hah, for being a ranch girl, she could clean up well occasionally.

Heading back in her room, she saw Clara was already there with the lipstick, some mascara, and eyeliner. Charity was relieved that it wasn't a set up for a full face like Cici loved to wear and Clara would occasionally sport, but also that her sister had even thought of it at all.

She wished that she could say the whole process went smoothly, but of course it didn't. If mascara was supposed to go on her eyes, why did the tiniest miss-stroke of that spiky little wand cause an instant rush of tears that caused all of it to run down her face?

But black tears and maybe a few choice words later, she was ready and actually looked quite nice, if she did say so herself. Those hypoallergenic makeup wipes of Clara's certainly did a wonder for mascara runs.

"How much longer?" Charity asked, reaching over to grab her phone and check the time.

"Don't worry. I set an alarm. You still have ten minutes before he's supposed to arrive."

"It's Alejandro, which means he'll be here in five minutes. Come on, let's go downstairs so he won't have to see me wobble down the stairs in wedges."

"You could always take the shoes off to go down the stairs."

"Nope," Charity answered, wiggling her toes. "I already put them on which means I'm married to them for the night. Any wavering in my devotion will let me wimp out later."

"Don't worry. You're going out to eat. That's not exactly a lot of time spent on your feet."

"Uh-huh. That's the only reason I'm allowing you to put me in them. Now, how about we take the lift?"

They did indeed end up using the wheelchair lift. Charity felt guilty about it until she heard Cass's pealing laughter fill the lower floor. Head turning this way and that, she finally spotted her sister sitting just in the entryway to the kitchen, doubled over the handle of the walker she'd been trying to use for very short distances as she laughed and laughed.

"Careful there, before you hurt yourself."

"Oh I, I... somebody get me my chair!"

The lift landed and Clara rushed to do just that. Charity, however, was a touch more reticent. "It wasn't *that* funny."

Cass calmed down enough to speak. "It's only funny because I know you. Only you would use my wheelchair lift to the second floor because of those baby wedge heels. I love it, I *love* it. People thinking we have this fancy thing for me, the invalid, but *nope*, it's to rescue you from two inches of lift!"

"Yeah, yeah," she muttered, but really, she was just so happy to see Cass laugh like that. "Make fun all you want, but once you're back to one hundred percent, I'll stick you in a pair of heels and see how well you do."

"Better than you, I hope."

"You're lucky that you're already in a wheelchair, otherwise those might be fighting words."

"Oh yeah, I can take you on like this, come at me, baby wedges."

Charity rolled her eyes before she cracked and laughed gently too. Man, it felt so good to mess around with her siblings again.

"I hear Alejandro on the steps," Clara said, jerking Charity to attention right before a knock sounded on the door.

It was time.

It was time.

"Any last-minute look critiques?" she asked nervously, looking to her sisters with panic.

"You're fine. You're beautiful," Clara assured, her broad, warm hands on Charity's shoulders. She was used to looking up to her sister, but with her heels on, they were eye to eye. And it was gazing straight on at her face that Charity realized just how much Clara looked like her mother.

Mama had never had a chance to take pictures before prom, or even meet Eric. And somehow, even though she very much knew the woman in front of her was Clara and not her late mother, it almost made her feel like maybe, just maybe, her mom was seeing her off anyway.

"I'll see the two of you later."

"A lot later, hopefully," Cass said with a grin. "Don't come back early on our account."

Another roll of her eyes and then Charity was headed to the door. She opened it, ready to greet Alejandro and say something witty, but then she *saw* Alejandro and all of that went out the window.

He was dressed in gray slacks with a fitted, plum button up and a black vest that looked like someone had crafted it just for him. And who knew, he was a doctor, so maybe he invested in a tailoring service. It wasn't like he had his own personal Clara to provide a last-minute wardrobe addition (that wasn't actually last minute). His hair was just as thick and shining as ever, but it definitely seemed like he had put some sort of product in it to style it more purposefully than usual. And in his hands was a beautiful but sensible bouquet of flowers, which he extended towards her.

"You look lovely tonight," he said, voice thick as she shakily took the flowers.

Oh goodness, she was about to go on a date. A real, honest-to-goodness date. He brought her *flowers*. The last time she'd gotten flowers was when she was twenty-one. Years ago.

"Right back at'cha," she said, complete with finger guns. Oh help, save her from herself.

"I'll go put these in water," Clara said, sweeping up behind Charity and saving the day. Thank God for her siblings, because she would be drowning without them. "You two have fun."

"Uh, yes. Thank you, Clara," Alejandro said, a sort of boyish charm to him as he offered Charity his arm. At least she could take comfort in the fact that he was just as out of his depth as she was, although he certainly looked quite dashing for being "out of his depth."

They headed to his car, and he only let go of her to open her door for her, closing it behind her. Huh, he was taking the whole gentleman thing pretty seriously. A small, brash part of her thought that she didn't need it. She was all hard edges and bad habits, after all. But another part of her preened at it, taking her back to a time when she'd been full of hope and naïve romantic notions.

It wasn't a long drive to the restaurant. Less than twelve minutes, but definitely too far to walk, especially in wedges. They didn't talk overly much in the car, clearly both of them nervous, but it wasn't a strained sort of silence either.

"What's Savannah up to, by the way?" she asked once they were almost there, the little girl popping up in the back of her mind. Sometimes it was easy to forget how young Savannah was and that she definitely needed a babysitter.

"One of Mrs. Whittaker's nieces who's an older teen is at the house with her. I was going to have her stay overnight with her great aunt and uncle, but then realized she would probably wear them out too much."

"Ah yes, they moved right after he retired, right? How are they liking that?"

"My aunt loves it. She says she finally has time to catch up with all the things she has to do and hobbies she wanted to try. But my uncle says he's going absolutely nuts."

"Ain't that the way it goes. I don't care how old I am, I'm going to be fixing and making things until they chuck me in the grave."

"Is that so?" he asked with that crooked sort of grin of his. While it was true that with Alejandro many of his emotions were... muted, that made Charity savor them that much more when she coaxed a genuine show out of him.

"Yup. Probably even make my coffin myself. You know what they say, if you want to do something right, the best way is to do it yourself."

"I might have heard that once or twice before."

"Uh-huh, I'm sure."

The lights of the restaurant's small parking lot came into view, and the next thing she knew, they were parking. This was it; she really was about to go into a restaurant and have her first real date in almost a decade. For a moment, Eric's words sneered in her ear, curling around her brain and sinking in until his oily hate was all she could hear. That she was mannish, disgusting, that he tolerated her for years, but she was just too *much* and yet not enough. That there was a reason God made it so she couldn't be a mother and no man would truly want her.

"Are you alright?"

"Huh?" She blinked and came back to the present, the cloud of her ex's words rolling back but still lingering at the edges of her mind. Alejandro had parked and was holding her door open again, hand extended. Oh, when had he done that? "Oh yeah, I'm fine. I was just thinking."

"Good things, I hope."

Now that was a dangerous question if there ever was one. "I'm surprised there aren't more cars here," she said instead, taking his hand and letting him help her out. She didn't need that either, but it was... *nice.* Everything about Alejandro was so *nice.* It was unfamiliar and lovely and also felt kind of like a trap. "Normally, Fridays at this place are pretty jam-packed."

"Are they usually?" he said it like he was surprised anything in their small town could be described as "jam-packed."

"Well yeah, I'm sure you've seen it yourself." She felt him stiffen slightly as they walked towards the entrance, and she turned her head to give him a sharper look. "Alejandro, you *have* gone out to eat at least once here, right? You've lived here almost three months. It's almost Halloween!"

"I don't get out much," was all he said, and Charity could hear the slight streak of sorrow below it.

"Well, that's alright," she comforted. "We're out now."

"That we are."

With that they were inside, and the hostess was greeting them. If she thought anything about the eldest Miller out with someone who wasn't her family, she didn't say anything. Then again, she was young enough that maybe she couldn't recognize any of the Miller family on sight. Ever since her divorce, Charity had basically withdrawn from almost all town life, and her siblings weren't exactly more active in the community either.

The hostess seated them in a booth over in a corner,

quickly but politely telling her their server's name, and then she was off.

"That was certainly amiable," Alejandro said without a hint of sarcasm to his voice.

"Really? That was kind of brusque compared to what the service normally is."

His eyebrows went up as if he wasn't sure if *she* was serious or not, but then he seemed to realize she was because he shook his head. "I guess I'm still used to the cadence of the city, in some ways."

"San Diego? Yeah, I bet things are more hurried there."

"In all ways except the traffic, probably."

If Charity had a drink, she would have choked on it. "*Is* it as bad as they say?"

"What, you've never been there yourself?"

"I'll be honest, the last time I went to a big city was New York City about six years ago and that was enough to last me a good long while." She shuddered as she remembered the close press of people. And how *loud* it was. How there were so many faces around her but not a single familiar soul and how everything smelled of urine or pot. Ugh.

Sure, there were lovely parts, like the fashion district and an aquarium, but she could never feel settled in that sort of environment. Always on edge as if she were waiting for something to happen.

"Well, maybe I can take you to San Diego sometime. Show you the zoo and some of my old stomping grounds. I think Savannah would be beside herself if she got to show you all her favorite animals."

Oh.

They were less than a half-hour into their date and he was talking about going out and taking her somewhere. That had to be a good thing, no matter how much her mind tried to take it apart and put it in a negative light.

But Alejandro must have interpreted her reaction as something else, because he was quickly trying to correct himself again. "I mean, not to put pressure on you or anything, I just, even if nothing comes of this, I still want to be friends."

Geez, the poor guy was so nervous. But Charity understood the feeling. She was so used to being assured of everything she did and sticking to what she knew, so doing something so completely out of her depths made her stomach clench and her blood bubble with an exhilarating and nauseating sort of excitement.

"Don't worry. If this... if this dating thing turns out to be not for us, I think we could be very good friends. Savannah certainly wouldn't mind."

He let out a breath of relief that Charity identified with, but then the waitress was there, and it was time to actually look at the menus.

She hadn't planned on ordering a drink, but Alejandro got himself a single dark lager and insisted that she get something if she wanted. That was how she ended up with an order of a large glass of water and even larger Top Shelf margarita to go with the endless chips and salsa. It wasn't enough to get her drunk, of course, she hated being even tipsy in public. But it was enough to add a warm sort of syrupiness to the edge of her nerves to make them less sharp and biting.

"So, what do you recommend here?"

"Honestly, all of it. The owners are first-generation and their food is really authentic. Or at least that's what I'm told. I'm not exactly an expert on the matter—I just like eating it."

"Alright, that's encouraging. Not that I don't trust your opinion, but some of my old coworkers would take me to 'authentic' places and..." He let out a puff of breath, his eyebrows shooting up. "...let's just say their reviews weren't exactly accurate."

Charity chuckled at that. "Don't worry, I don't hold any illusions about my expertise."

"Good to know." They looked at the menu for a few moments, and Charity felt a surge of insecurity she wasn't used to. She normally ordered two entrees so she could eat herself silly and then take some leftovers home, but that felt... gluttonous to do right in front of her date.

"This all looks like it could be delicious. Why don't I just order the dinner for four and we eat ourselves silly and take the rest home? If this is as good as you say it is, Savannah will be distraught if I don't bring her at least one container home."

He was just *too* good.

"You said exactly what was on my mind."

"Hah, did I? Good, I hate when people get all prim and proper about food. I think because I'm a doctor, some folks assume I'm going to judge them for taking in more than their usual daily caloric intake."

"Well, a lot of doctors are *real* judgey about weight. Clara is one of the healthiest and strongest people I know, but until she started going to your uncle, they always tried to get her to diet to lose weight."

Alejandro frowned at that, and Charity felt relief wash through her. She was incredibly protective of Clara and if he was dismissive or judgmental of her, she would have ended the date right then and there.

"Clara? I'm sorry. There's a lot of... bias in the medical community. In a lot of different ways. It's one of the reasons I decided to switch from PT to becoming an MD. I felt like I could make more of a difference that way."

"I... I didn't know that. That's really cool."

He shrugged, that light dusting of color on his cheeks again. Did he get that way with all compliments, or just ones from her? "It's nothing to brag about. Or at least it shouldn't be. Our oath means we should be providing equal care to all, no exceptions."

"I understand what you mean. During the summer we hire a seasonal ranch hand or two, and sometimes certain town folks have *opinions* on who we hire."

She didn't have to elaborate; he knew exactly what she meant. It was nice, how easily the communication flowed between them once they stopped letting their nerves drive them.

The conversation fell into something easier while they waited for their food, but they barely had fifteen minutes of chit-chat and her margarita was still half-full when their meals started coming out.

And boy was it a *lot*.

Charity had ordered the meal for three once when she and two of her siblings were there, but it had nothing on the meal for four. Apparently, that extra person was supposed to be *real* hungry, because there were two extra entrees along with two extra sides and a whole stack of additional tortillas.

Delicious.

The conversation lulled as they began to stuff their faces. It wasn't quite barbaric, but after a moment of watching Alejandro load his plate up, she dug in too. She did watch him carefully, however, to see what he thought of the fare, and pretty much from the first *mmm*, it was clear that he liked it.

Victory. She always felt a bit of pride whenever someone liked her food, restaurant, or seed recommendations.

"This is *good*," Alejandro said after they demolished at least a quarter of it. "This is *so good*."

"Glad to see my stomach knows what it's talking about."

"Remind me to never doubt you."

"Probably a good habit to get into."

He laughed at that, pausing in their eating to sip at his beer. He had an easy smile on his face and his shoulders weren't up by his ears anymore. He seemed more relaxed than she'd ever seen him—the wonders that a belly full of delicious food and a cozy atmosphere could do.

"Savannah's probably going to force me to come here at least once a week."

"Goodness, bringing her to the ranch once a week, coming here once a week. Taking me on a trip to San Diego. If you're not careful, you might accidentally develop a social life."

He huffed a laugh at that, not quite bitter, but perhaps a little too real. "I don't think we're in danger of that anytime soon. I've lived here for months now and my only friends are, well, you and Mrs. Whittaker. Although Savannah is quite taken with her school librarian as well."

"Hmmm, that's... Miss Edelira, right?"

"You know her?"

"No, not much. But I met her at your party while she and Papa were playing cards. She seemed to be a lovely lady."

Alejandro's eyes narrowed at her and she shot him back a similar look.

"What?" she asked.

"You have a tone."

"What, I don't have a tone."

"You *absolutely* have a tone."

Okay, maybe she had the *slightest* bit of a tone. "It's nothing, really. I just noticed that they seemed to be having a good time and played cards for a while. Is it so wrong for a woman to want her Papa to have someone? It's been over a decade, you know, he deserves not to be lonely anymore."

A rapid series of micro-expressions crossed Alejandro's face before he settled on a softer grin, his eyes a bit hazy. Maybe even misty? But that didn't even make sense. "You think so?"

"I know so." It was heavy conversation for dinner, but Alejandro asked, and he just looked so *vulnerable*, all raw around the edges like he might unravel right then and there. "If anyone understands grieving, it's me. Losing mom was like losing my anchor in the world." His face went funny at that again, so she hurried to explain. "Papa is wonderful, but he's always been a dreamer. Mama was the one who had him hire a financial planner to make sure he wasn't just blowing through his inheritance. She's the one who planned out much of the ranch, and she had so many more ideas for our homestead.

"Papa helped her believe in herself, he championed her, but she was always the one willing to forge ahead into new things. And when she was gone, we all... well, we were all lost. Our de facto leader had disappeared in chunks and we all had to figure out what to do.

"I get that he needed years. *I* needed years, and she was his soulmate. But then we all left high school. And then all of us were in our twenties. And now it's been over a decade and I *know* he's lonely, that he's missing that companionship, but he refuses to even acknowledge it.

"So yeah, I see him smiling at a sweet older lady and having a good time, and maybe my mind runs away with itself. But still, I can't help... I can't help but have hope for him, even if he doesn't have any."

Alejandro didn't answer for a moment, and when he did, his voice was thick. It was only then that Charity realized just how much his situation tended to mirror her father's, and she could have kicked herself for not seeing it. "I... I think I'm beginning to see what you mean. And... why you might feel that way."

His tone was so raw, and when his eyes flicked up to her from the food, she saw the fear there. The worry. The uncertainty. And instead of offending her or scaring her off, it made her feel closer to him than ever. Emotions were so strange.

"I'm glad I make at least some sense to you."

Slowly, one of his hands moved over the table, until it was hovering over where she'd been resting hers. She watched, heart in her throat, as he tentatively let it rest on top of hers, his fingers brushing against her skin and sending electricity zinging up her arm.

"You're one of the few things in the world that just makes sense to me."

Each of those words hit her like an arrow, going straight to her heart and making her *ache* with the flood of emotions. Good, bad, happy, fearful, it all blended together in a heavy rush that had her reaching for her water to gulp it down until she got her head right.

She ended up running out of water first, sadly, and when she set down her empty cup, she realized Alejandro's hand was still over hers, warm and wonderful and perfect.

It was silly; she was a thirty-two-year-old woman going off about some very PG hand-holding like a middle schooler, but it was what it was. It had been so *long*. Not that there weren't the occasional interested party, but after Eric... well, she could never lower her defensive walls long enough to even care about trying to date any of them.

But Alejandro was different. And maybe he was just different because Savannah came in swinging with that sledgehammer of hers, knocking over barriers right and left and encouraging Charity to daydream about all those things she'd given up for herself. Leaving her a bit more open, a bit more exposed, just enough for Charity to acknowledge that she was attracted to Alejandro.

"You're a very nice man, Alejandro."

"But?"

"Why a but?"

"Those kinds of sentences almost always have a but. 'You're a very nice man, Alejandro, but you're always so shut off. You're doing well, Alejandro, but you're just going through the motions. You're a good father, Alejandro, but you can't be a mother.' It's a conjunction I'm pretty familiar with."

Each of those sentences bit at her and she wanted to brawl with whoever had told him all that. Alejandro already had so much on his plate, more than a parent should ever have, and people making him feel bad about his grieving was such a low, scummy thing to do.

"No, no buts. I was just stating a fact because I wanted to."

He seemed surprised by that, huffing out a soft laugh. "I'm not used to that."

"Well, get used to it, because if you stick around, I intend to do that a lot."

He swallowed more of his beer, but suddenly his eyes were staring at her with that intense expression again, the one that made her fill with heat just as much as it did nerves. "I do plan to stick around, if you let me."

Words didn't come to her immediately, but when they did, they were careful. She felt like she was walking along the edge of a precipice, always one step away from saying too much and tumbling over the edge into some sort of catastrophic end.

"I'd like that," she managed finally.

And that was that. The words were out. She admitted something she wanted, despite life teaching her that the moment she did that it would snatch whatever she was hoping for away from her.

The moment, however, was interrupted when their server came by to ask them how the food was, reminding them about the spread they had under them, and Alejandro asked for two to-go boxes the next time the server came around. Then they were both digging in again.

The conversation flowed in and out, never going quite as deep or heavy as before, but still lovely. Charity felt like she was flying, drunk on the comfort and ease of it all instead of the margarita. Sure, it warmed her, maybe lowered her clenched fist around her feelings, but she knew what was going on inside of her was entirely of her own doing. The rushing feeling below her skin, the way her heart was thumping, how she felt hyperaware of Alejandro's every move and word.

Before she knew it, the server brought the check, then returned twice more to see if there was anything more they needed. Fishing her phone out of her dress's pocket—it had pockets!—she realized it was almost time for the family restaurant to close.

"Where did the time go?"

"What do you—"

She showed Alejandro her phone and his eyes went wide.

"There's no way that's possible. We haven't been here for three hours."

"Unless we were randomly in a time jump and didn't know it, yeah, we have."

He shook his head, but he was still grinning. "Insane, I had no idea. Well, we better hurry up and clear out before they kick us out."

"Yeah, we don't want to burn a bridge at one of the two restaurants in our town." But as they hurriedly divvied up the leftovers, Charity couldn't help but feel the slightest bit melancholy. It was like they'd created a perfect little bubble around themselves, no one else to bother them and no other obligations. Just the two of them getting over their nerves bit by bit.

"I... I wish that this didn't have to end. This is the most fun I've had in ages," she said.

Alejandro paused, looking at her with that intense expression *again*. She was beginning to think that there was so much to the man that was carefully kept behind a thick veneer, like he was afraid that if he let himself feel like a human, all the emotions he was burying would just explode out and overwhelm him.

"Why does it have to?"

"Huh?" Oh, eloquent. She was about as smooth as granulated butter.

"We're both adults and it's the weekend, Savannah is taken care of, and we both have licenses. We can stay up as late as we want, go wherever we want to go."

...oh.

He was right. She was thirty-two, but the idea stood so foreign in her head. Foreign, but not unwelcome. It took a moment, but then a giddy sort of laugh bubbled up from her as she realized just how right he was.

"You got any bug spray in your car?"

"Huh?" Hey, at least he was just about as eloquent as her.

"Bug spray, you got it?"

"Yes, why?"

"There's this really pretty spot me n' Cass used to go to a bit away from here off a hiking trail. It's by this mini-waterfall, but a lot of mosquitos love it at night, so it's best to be prepared."

"You're going to show me your secret sibling hideout?" he asked, that crooked grin right back in place.

"That depends, bug spray or no?"

"Yes, I have bug spray. Never much been a friend of being eaten, so I put some in my glove compartment for every time I visit your ranch."

"Clever man."

"I try. My mom says I could even be a doctor one day."

"Hmm, I wouldn't believe everything your mama says."

He barked out a laugh at that, pulling money from his wallet and placing it on the table. Charity was about to protest that she could pay for the meal and ten times over without even noticing its absence, but quickly shut her mouth. He was doing something *nice* for her. The proper response was "thank you."

But then he was tugging her out the door, their to-go boxes under her arm, and she didn't get a chance to say that either.

She didn't mind though, still floating on the cloud that came from a good meal with good company. It was like a dream, but better, and like Alejandro said, the night could last as long as they wanted it to.

19

Alejandro

Charity did not play fair.

He should have known that from what time they did spend together, but when she opened that door in a green number with her hair wound about her head like royalty, it was like his heart had stopped right there in his chest.

She looked... *perfect*. The neckline of the emerald dress was somewhere between conservative and alluring, his eyes going to her décolletage and the ranch-tanned skin there. There were a few silvery-white scars across her collarbone, barely visible, but enough to make him wonder. And she was wearing the shortest sleeves he'd ever seen her in, revealing perfectly toned, muscular arms from all her work on the ranch.

The dress was fitted at the top and flared at her waist, and he realized that they were almost eye to eye. Somehow, he managed not to stare right then and there, but when she walked to the car, his gaze slid along her bare legs. They were shapely and strong.

That was *not* a good line of thought, this was only their first date and he was a respectable man—*whew*, Charity Miller did *not* play fair.

She was beautiful and young and smart and so funny it was hard for him not to feel outclassed by her in every way possible. He knew others might think differently, considering that he was a doctor and she was a rancher, but they were wrong. Charity was so much *more*.

Then there was dinner, and without knowing it, she'd talked about exactly what he needed to hear. It was easy to forget that she'd grown up without a mother—she was so well adjusted after all. But when she'd sat there, looking at him with that vulnerable, open expression as she said how she felt about her Papa, well, it was so easy to understand how Savannah probably felt, or would feel eventually.

And he didn't want Savannah to feel like that. He didn't want her to worry about him or wish he moved on. He didn't want her to fret about him being lonely or incomplete. There was still so much weighing him down, so much to change and examine, but he found it a little easier to loosen his grip on that anchor deep inside of him.

It had been too good to be true, from the food to her company to *everything*, but then she said she wanted *more*, and that was how Alejandro found himself pulling into a small parking lot beside a rocky face with thick trees on top.

It looked somewhat ominous to him, but Charity was already out of his car and heading forward, her cell phone shining bright to lead her way.

"Are you sure this is safe since you're in heels and all?" he asked, hurrying to catch up with her. He wasn't *scared* per se, but he knew enough what a rolled or twisted ankle could do, and there was already one Miller child out of action. Considering how much Charity did for her family, they would definitely get behind if she was out of commission for even a week.

"Oh, the path's so worn that I could walk along here in stilts and probably be fine."

"You know how to walk on stilts?"

"Well, no. But I could still probably do it."

Alejandro couldn't help but chuckle at the fierce determination as her chin jutted forward. "If anyone could be naturally good at it, it's you."

"You don't need to butter me up, I'm already on a date with you."

"That's true, but I've heard that being nice increases the chances of you wanting to do this whole thing with me again."

"Hmm, sounds fake."

They shared a laugh at that and before he really thought about it, he was reaching for her hand. She didn't resist at all, instead interlocking her fingers with him and smiling so sweetly at him that he felt like he could float away.

"Come on, it's this way. It'll be worth it, I promise," Charity said.

"I trust you."

And he did. He had barely met the woman, but he trusted her. Maybe it was because Savannah was so steadfast in her devotion towards the cowgirl, or maybe it was just something about Charity that was irresistible. He didn't particularly care either way. The only thing that mattered was he felt at ease with her in a way he hadn't in so long that the sensation was all but forgotten.

"I... okay."

They were quiet as they moved through the trees, and he couldn't help but compare the little walk to something out of a horror movie. He wasn't *averse* to nature. He actually quite liked hikes. But being in a new state in an unknown park at night definitely had some dangerous vibes to it.

Eventually, however, Charity must have sensed his nerves, because she started talking about different high school stories of her and her sister and how they'd run away to the spot. Nothing salacious, not even close, but it was fun to imagine young and uncertain Charity. Was she ever not the put together, strong woman that she was now? Like she loved to say so often, "sounds fake."

He heard it first, the pounding, churning thrum of a waterfall doing its thing. He tried to look around in the darkness, seeing if he could spot its location, but the only thing he could really see was the narrow slice of nature that was illuminated by Charity's cellphone light.

But eventually, the path leveled out and the trees thinned, then they were walking into a neat little clearing with a thick creek running through it. It *was* pretty, with several large, flat rocks that were set up as seats and what was clearly a fire circle.

"So, this is your little hideaway, huh?"

Charity nodded. "Yup. Try not to be so impressed." He opened his mouth to object that he wasn't *not* impressed before realizing that she was teasing him. Cheeky.

But that was one of the things he found himself liking about her. Charity was unpredictable, kept him on his toes, and after a carefully curated sort of existence, that kind of change was heady.

Terrifying.

But also, heady.

She moved over to one of the rocks and settled on it, her skirt pulling up and fanning out at the motion. He tried not to notice, but he was a man and she was *so* beautiful, so how was he supposed to *not* notice.

It was like he was acutely aware of how much of a woman she was, her intense, cat-like eyes, to her strength, to the dips and swells of her figure. The last time he'd ever deigned to look at a woman like that, she'd been his wife.

Yeah, definitely terrifying. He felt the fear, the guilt biting at him, threatening to pull him back under. And it would be *so* easy to slip. All he had to do was listen to the voice telling him that he was betraying Tirza and that would be it.

But instead, he sat down next to her.

It was hardly an illicit touch. Their arms pressed against each other and that was it, but it still had his blood simmering, shooting through his veins like it was lightning.

Actually, after treating Nathan for a couple weeks, he'd rather not have anything to do with lightning.

"When I was younger, I used to feel my mother in this place."

Alejandro blinked back to the present. "Your mother?"

She nodded, her head tilting upwards just like she did when they were standing on her porch. "Like most kids, I thought heaven was actually in the sky. So when I looked up there, I guessed that she had to be one of the stars looking down at me. Clichéd, I know."

He replied without thinking, the usual chorus of doubts having no time to kick up. "No, I think that's beautiful."

She smiled weakly, but her eyes never left the sky. "Cass and I would write her letters and burn them in that fire pit. For a while, anyway."

"Did something change?"

"Yeah. We got older. Realized heaven wasn't actually in the sky, but something more abstract than that."

"What do you think heaven is?"

Now she actually did look at him, the corner of her mouth lifting slightly. "Aren't you supposed to not talk about politics or religion on a first date?"

Alejandro just shrugged. Maybe, but the urge to comfort Charity, to know what really was on her mind, went far beyond caring about any faux politeness. "We've already talked about so much. Religion seems like a natural progression."

She chuckled at that, but the sound was so dry it could have almost been a cough. Alejandro didn't say anything, however, giving her the time to say whatever it was she wanted to.

"I guess I think heaven is somewhere between a different dimension but also all around us. And sometimes, when those layers are especially close, we can *just* brush up against the edge of it and you can *feel* it.

"Whether it's when you're riding your horse as the sun is rising and you stop to watch it appear over the hills. Or sometimes maybe when you're watching a bee flit from flower to flower. Maybe you feel it when you see the smile of someone you love.

"I used to look for those moments. Hunt them down even. But the worst way to find heaven is to look for it."

"What is the best way to find it?"

Finally, her gaze turned fully to him and there was so *much* there in the depths. It overwhelmed him, but it invigorated him at the same time. He wanted to feel everything she was, to hear every thought out of her mind and memorize it.

"To live. To love. To just enjoy and be grateful for life." Then that look grew bitter and her eyes went back to the sky. "But you have to be open to *feeling* too, which can be hard to do when everything *hurts* so much."

The way her voice broke at that, and her head turned away from him. It tore through Alejandro, and he felt the urge to protect rise in his chest.

"Charity," he murmured.

She didn't look towards him, so he gently reached towards her, gently turning her head so he could see her face. Her eyes were red-rimmed and misty, as if she needed to cry but refused to let herself.

It was a shame, really, how strong she clearly felt she had to be all the time. Tirza had been much the same way for a long time. One of the things that attracted him to women was also something that could lead them to so much pain.

"That's the best description of heaven I've ever heard."

"Really?" she asked, so uncertainly that his heart ached. "Most people just seem to humor me."

"Well, maybe because those people haven't felt those little slices of heaven."

"And you have?" she asked.

The starlight was in her eyes again, shimmering and bright, thousands of promises, dreams and hopes. Alejandro brought his other hand up to cup her face, his thumbs stroking that beautiful bone structure of hers. And he knew how strong she was, how fierce, so the fact that she just *let* him, made his blood rush and his heart thunder.

"Of course. I'm holding one right now."

The soft gasp of hers jolted through his soul, and his entire attention went to the way those perfect, ruby lips of hers parted slightly. He was caught up in the rush of it all, the rush of her, and without thinking he rushed it.

It was only at the very last second that he stopped, realizing that—no matter how much he wanted to kiss her—he hadn't asked permission and it was only their first date. He looked down at Charity, who was staring at him with wide eyes, her pupils so wide that her gaze was almost black.

"Can I—" he started to ask; their faces so close that his lips just barely ghosted over hers as he spoke. But then one of her hands was in his hair, one of her hands was on his shoulder, and she was yanking him closer until their lips collided together.

Oh.

It was heat and desire, raw and open with unfinished edges. It bit at him, but he welcomed the sharp scrape of the rush, his hands leaving Charity's face to glide down her neck, then onto her shoulders. He wanted to hold her, to protect her and let the soft femininity of her come to the surface. He wanted to learn every bit of her, and it was like a tidal wave that swept over him and washed him away.

He hadn't kissed someone in eight years, and what a kiss to come back on. She was demanding, urgent, borderline desperate, but so was he. They held each other like they weren't sure whether to push each other away or pull closer.

But he wanted to be closer, *needed* to be closer, and she must have felt it too. He wanted to feel her heartbeat against his chest, wanted to be able to put a finger on her pulse and feel it flutter just for him.

And Charity, beautiful, powerful, relentless Charity hugged him back.

Heat. *Heat.* So much rushing through him.

Some part of Alejandro was aware that he needed to stop.

That they were rushing too fast, too wildly towards something neither of them discussed. There was so much to talk about. He figured she was a Christian, but he didn't know how she felt about such things. And he was aware that people looked at him and had certain... assumptions.

But he'd only slept with one woman in his entire life, and that woman was the girl he'd dated since his freshman year of college and married. If Charity expected some sort of Casanova, then she was mistaken.

But also... part of him almost wanted to be that type of person if only it meant that Charity stayed in his arms, letting him hold her, *kiss* her.

No, they needed to stop. They *needed* to.

But still, but still...

He could feel himself slipping to the thrill of it, the comfort it felt to be touched, to be desired, and to desire someone else. He'd shut himself off from everything for so long that he'd forgotten how to deal with them. It filled his head, his body, until there was nothing left but the want, the want, the *want*.

Until, of course, Charity suddenly stiffened.

Like someone dumped a bucket of ice over his head, that debate stopped in its tracks and he pulled away to look up at her face. Her expression was crumpled, her eyes closed.

He'd ruined her lipstick, smearing it around her lips, and he had no doubt that his face was equally stained. But that didn't matter, not when she looked so close to breaking in his grasp.

"Charity? Are you okay?"

"No! I mean, yes. I'm just..." She took a shaky breath but then that cracked, and she was pressing her palms to her face. "I'm lying to you."

"What?" was all he could say, because what on earth could *that* mean? "What are you talking about? Charity look at me, please?" What had he done? He'd been so *selfish!* He had ruined it, getting so swept up in everything. What was he thinking?

Her hands dropped enough for her watery eyes to look at him. "I'm sorry. I just... I'm sorry."

He gripped her wrists lightly, his thumbs stroking the skin there. "Charity, please tell me what's wrong. What do you think you're lying about?"

"Myself, Alejandro. Myself! I'm sitting here, pretending like I could deserve someone like you, but if I tell you even half the things about my past that you've told me about yours, you'd know..."

He swallowed hard. "I'd know what, Charity?"

The pain on her face, the pure agony, made his own eyes start to water. She was *hurting.* He hated it. He wanted to wrap her in blankets and hold her closely while feeding her the nicest chocolates until she forgot about everything that could possibly be upsetting her.

"...that I'm damaged goods. That someone like you wanting to date someone like me is ridiculous."

That was it; his heart was breaking. Not for himself, but for whatever awful thing that could possibly make a creative, determined woman like Charity think something so awful. "Someone like me, Charity? You think I'm somehow better than you?"

"I don't think! I *know!* You're this successful doctor and single father who always does right by everyone. You gave up working in a successful practice in San Diego to come to this small town and help us. Because of you, your uncle was finally able to retire and enjoy himself for once.

"You're kind to everyone. You *listen*. You never judge. You had the love of your life stolen from you and you're not bitter or angry about it, and here I am, fighting to hold back all this rage all the time and barely winning."

"I—"

"I'm not a doctor. I don't have any job, really. And I didn't lose my first love to some awful disease; he *left* me. He divorced me after I found him in the arms of his 'business' partner because I couldn't give him what he wanted.

"Because there's something *wrong* with me. I can't have children. I couldn't give him what he wanted, what everybody wants, because for some reason God decided that I wouldn't be a good mother. I'm damaged, intrinsically, and you deserve someone better than that."

That was so much to parse out, and Alejandro felt his brain spinning to do so. Charity had been married before. And the man had left her because she couldn't bear his children?

So many comments from her Papa, from her siblings, and even himself played through his head in rapid succession, and he suddenly realized just how much subtext he'd missed.

"I can't force you to do anything, but I will warn you, if you start to play a will-they-won't-they game with my sister after everything she's been through, we'll see just how type A I can go on your kneecaps."

"Having half of your heart ripped out when you were so sure that you'd have it forever."

· · ·

"I LOVE MY GIRL, I do, but the truth is she's gone through some things that have hurt her. Real bad. She tries to hide it, pretend that she's alright, but a father knows, you know?"

IT HAD BEEN RIGHT THERE the whole time, the clues laid out like billboards. But he'd been so obsessed with his own melodrama that he hadn't taken the time to think about *hers*.

And suddenly, anger burned through him. Anger at himself, but a whole lot of anger at whatever scummy ex-husband she had who had wounded her so terribly. She didn't deserve that in the slightest. No, she deserved to be valued and cherished and shown just how incredibly wonderful she was.

"I'm a thirty-something divorcée with no ambitions or prospects. I'm... I'm just..."

He caught her face in his hands again, urging her to look at him. She did, her words trailing off as his thumbs wiped at her tears. "You're just perfect, to me," he whispered, hoping she could feel exactly how much he meant it.

"How could you say that?" She breathed raggedly, like if the wrong words came out of his mouth that she just might tumble apart in his hands.

"Because it's true, absolutely true." He knew he needed to open himself, to be honest in a way he hadn't for almost a decade. He needed to stop being afraid. "You are one of the kindest people I know. The way Savannah lights up when she's beside you is otherworldly. And you're brilliant in a way I can't even understand. I've seen the things that you've built, and it blows my mind every time.

"I've seen you fiercely protect everyone who's close to you.

You're hilarious, you're beautiful, and you've lived through traumas that some people have nightmares about.

"The only thing that's ridiculous is the idea that you somehow aren't good enough for me. *I'm* the coward. I'm so afraid of facing so many things that I've nearly tanked any chance of us ever happening multiple times. *I'm* the one who's not good for you."

She was staring at him like she couldn't believe what he was saying, but he desperately wanted her to. He wanted her to see how brilliant she was. How she was the one person besides his daughter who'd made life worth living since Tirza closed her eyes for the last time.

And she wasn't a replacement for Tirza. No, not at all. That would be an insult for them both. She was something new, powerful, and terrifying all at the same time. She was a second chance, exactly who and what Tirza had begged him to leave himself open to.

"As for your ex? Obviously, an idiot and a scumbag. I can't begin to imagine what it's like to find out your body made a decision for you against your will, but there's more than one way to have a family. My father was adopted, you know, and he always taught me that family is who we decide our family to be. So, don't you dare let anybody tell you you're lesser, or damaged, because of any of that. You are a beautiful, amazing woman, Charity Miller, and I... I... you make me want to live in a way I didn't think was possible for me anymore."

She stared at him, those cat-like eyes wide and red, and then she was sobbing into the crook of his neck. And he held her, he held her and hurt for her, listening as she cried herself out.

"It's alright. I'm here. I'm gonna stay here," he said.

And he was. He was present in the moment, no slipping

away, no letting the anchor drag him down. He was as present as ever and not running away from any of it.

He couldn't say how long they stayed like that, her huddled against him, crying into his neck and shoulder.

It was intimate, so very intimate, but not in a sexual way. Something deeper, that touched his soul and made him want to wipe her tears when she was done and make sure she never cried again.

He was falling. He was falling hard and fast, and for once, he didn't want to run away from it.

Eventually, however, Charity muttered something into his skin that he couldn't understand.

"I'm sorry, what was that, *miha*?"

The slightest shiver went down her back under his hands, but he didn't comment on it as she sat up. "I'm being eaten alive by mosquitos. The spray must be wearing off."

Alejandro had been so tuned in to her and the situation that he hadn't noticed he had several points of itchiness along his hands and arms.

"Uh, you might just be right about that. Shall we head back?"

She nodded, wiping her face, then stood. Her wobbly legs had him reaching out for her, and he nearly preened when she easily wrapped her arms around his, letting him lead most of the way back.

They were relatively quiet up until they pulled up to her house. He opened her door, feeling that fear begin to seep back in. It was so much easier to be brave beside that loud mini fall, with the wild stars above them. But even if it was harder, he was going to try. She deserved that much, and so did Savannah. And Tirza.

And *him.*

"I know this wasn't a typical first date," he said as he led her to the front door. Her eyes looked less like she'd been sobbing her brains out, but there was still a sort of fragility to her. "But I'm really glad we did it."

They reached the door, and he could see the warm, buttery light of her living room and entryway spilling out into the night. Their date was over, and what a wild ride it'd been.

Would they both still feel the same in the morning? Or would the dawn of a new day erase everything like a spell that was never meant to last? Because so much of the situation seemed like an impossible dream or magic spell, something that was beautiful in the moment but couldn't last beyond the moment.

Or maybe it was just because he was so scared in believing in anything good because so much good had been stolen from him.

Wordlessly, Charity opened the door. He was so certain that that would be that, but then she turned at the last moment and pressed a kiss to his cheek.

"Thank you," she whispered, gazing up at him with that *look* again. "For everything."

"O-of course," he said, aware that his voice was dropping lower into that gravelly thrall that happened whenever he felt that rush of adrenaline and desire in him. "I do hope to take you out again. There's a whole nother restaurant in town, after all."

"You can count on it," she said with a wan smile before stepping inside. "I'll see you, Alejandro."

"Yeah, you will."

20

Alejandro

_L_ogically, Alejandro knew that he drove home, but in every other way, he felt like he just floated there. If someone asked him to describe his drive, he wouldn't have been able to, but he could describe just about everything from the date. The richness of the food Charity recommended thick on his tongue and warm in his stomach. The way he'd tasted it again as they kissed, wild and wanton and rushing.

How her body had leaned against him as she'd cried, trusting him with a state that was so vulnerable for her. Letting him see her when she was weak, when she was hurting. How she let him comfort her.

And how she looked standing in her doorway, the warm light of her house silhouetting her like a halo, looking at him like he _was_ someone worthy of her.

It was impossible. It was wonderful. It was everything that he'd never dared to let himself dream of, and it was right about when he stepped onto the porch that he realized it would be *so* easy to lose it.

She could die. He could die. They could break up. She could come to her senses and realize that she deserved something so much better.

And it wasn't like she was even in love with him yet. He was falling so hard and so fast, but all they'd done was kiss.

Granted, he'd fallen in love with Tirza the moment she kicked the man who'd stolen her bag, so there was kind of a precedent.

Alejandro was well aware that he was self-sabotaging like he always did as he walked into his house. He needed to focus on the good and stop letting that anchor of fear and coldness drag him back down.

The babysitter said things went great and that Savannah was up in her room asleep. The older teen looked wiped out from a night with his high energy daughter. Alejandro paid the babysitter well, thanked her, and made sure she got into her car and on her way safely.

Another light suddenly flicked on and Alejandro literally jumped. Then he spotted Savannah sitting on the couch with the light-remote in her hand. She must have snuck downstairs when she heard him arrive home.

"Look who's finally home," she said with a cheeky grin.

Alejandro looked to his watch, which told him it was almost midnight. "What are you doing up this late?"

"Did you really think I was gonna be able to sleep when my dad was on his very first date of my entire life?"

"... you may have a point." He stood there for a moment

before walking to her and handing her the to-go boxes. "You might want to heat bits of this up."

"Oh yay! Food!" She hopped up off the couch and ran it to the fridge. "I'll eat some in the morning. For now, tell me all about your date. Was it good? You were gone a long time, so it had to be good, right? Also, there's red, like, *all* over your face."

"Really?" He strode to the hallway mirror and *yup,* just like he'd thought. Charity's lipstick was smeared all around his mouth and chin. Seeing it there reminded him of just how intense that kiss had been, both of them searching for things that they'd denied ourselves for so long.

"Here, I got you a paper towel. You can tell me all about the date while you wipe off."

"You're awfully invested in this," he joked, taking the damp cloth and starting to scrub at his face. It didn't work overly well, but it was better than nothing.

"Why wouldn't I be? I like Charity, I like her family, and I like going to their ranch all the time."

Alejandro just reached over and ruffled her hair, but then she kept going. "And since I like all that, maybe I'd like her as a mom too."

That just about jolted right down Alejandro's spine. "You what now?"

She caught his tone, because of course she did. He and his daughter knew each other like the back of their hands. "Don't freak. I *know* it's too soon to tell—I'm not a *child.*"

"You actually are literally a child."

"*Dad!*" She gave him a flustered look and he held up his hands.

"Sorry. You were saying?"

"What I was *saying* was, I get that we can't know if she could be my new mom yet, but you can know *real* fast if she's *not.* So, I figure if the date went well, there's still a possibility. Besides…" Her face softened, and she looked up at him the same way she'd looked up at him when she was born, when she first learned to walk, and when he'd gotten his first big promotion. Like he was someone so *good* and important. "I like that she makes you smile a lot. You look happy now, Dad, and I don't want that to go away."

How could he argue with logic like that? Especially when it made his heart swell with how much love he had for his daughter.

"Yeah, she does make me smile a lot. And the date was… eventful, but good."

"And you're gonna date again?"

"She said she was amenable to the idea."

"Amenable? Like… hotel amenities?"

Alejandro chuckled. "I'm sure those sound similar for a reason, but amenable means she's open to it."

"Ah, that's good then." She jumped up, pressing a kiss to his opposite cheek that resulted in her ramming her face into his. "I guess I should go to bed then."

She started to head up the stairs, stretching and yawning. Alejandro watched her, but before she could disappear around the corner of the stairwell, he realized that he didn't want to go to sleep himself and didn't want to be alone.

"Savannah?"

"Yeah, Dad?"

"If you're not too tired, do you want to stay up, maybe watch a movie on the couch and eat some of that ice cream we bought?"

Her eyes widened like a child's did when they were excited, but then uncertainty flickered. "It'll ruin my bedtime."

"I know. You don't have to if you don't want to."

But then she turned around and skipped right back down the stairs. "I mean, if you're gonna *insist*, I suppose I could spare some of my valuable time."

"Your generosity knows no bounds."

"Yes, yes, you are correct. Can I pick out the movie?"

"Sure. I'll go grab the ice cream."

She let out a squeal and clapped her hands. It was a wonder she had so much energy even though it was significantly past her bedtime, and he wondered if she had napped while he was gone.

Or maybe she was just a kid, and kids tended to have boundless amounts of energy.

Either way, the two of them ended up curled on the couch together, eating their dessert as they watched one of her favorite movies about elves and monsters and dwarves. It was something they hadn't done in a while considering how busy he was, and it was the perfect way to end his day.

And for once, he wasn't scared of what the future might bring.

21

———————

Charity

"So, are you off on another date with Alejandro?"

Charity looked up from her vanity, where she was checking her hair one last time, to see Clara standing in the doorway, Cass right beside her with her walker. It had been a week since her and Alejandro's last date, and she almost couldn't believe how amazing things were going.

When she'd woken up the day after their first date, she'd been sure that she'd dreamed it all, or that Alejandro would think better of her emotional outburst and decide that she was crazy. Sure, he'd *said* nice things, that biological children didn't matter to him, and that he wasn't good enough for *her*, but that didn't mean he *meant* them.

But then there'd been a text waiting for her when she was finished with her first round of morning chores, wishing her a good morning and hoping she slept well. He and Savannah had apparently crashed on the couch, passed out after staying up too late after watching movies and binging on ice cream, so she probably wouldn't be stopping by that day but wanted to know if Sunday would work. It sounded like a good way to end the night to her, and she'd been smiling to herself as she quickly answered back.

Seeing him on Sunday was surprisingly nerve-racking, but after a few minutes, both of them relaxed and they were able to just *be* in each other's presence. Savannah was excited to try horseback riding again, and they spent several hours with their nicest, tiniest pony: Lilliputian, or Lilli for short.

Clara cooked dinner, as was quickly becoming the usual, and if she and Cass shared a few knowing looks, no one said anything.

"Yeah, I am," she said with a grin. "We're trying out the other restaurant in town."

"That's not bad. Two dates, two Fridays in a row. It's almost like you like him."

"Watch it," Charity warned, pointing her brush at her younger sister. "You may be bigger than me, but I can still tan your hide."

"I'll allow you to think that only because I like you."

"Exactly." Charity went back to finishing up pinning a wave of hair that was loose. But when she was done, she realized her sister hadn't moved. "What?"

"It's good to see you happy, that's all."

"It's good to be happy. Scary. But good."

She nodded, grinning from ear to ear, then headed off. Charity herself finished getting ready and headed downstairs. The last thing she wanted was to miss a single moment on her second date since her early twenties.

It finally felt like she could have all of the things she'd

been telling herself she couldn't for ages, and she desperately hoped she was right.

THE SECOND DATE went by just as brilliantly as the first, but with less crying and less out of control, desperate kissing in the middle of a hiking trail. Not that Charity didn't think about kissing Alejandro *a lot*, but after everything that had happened with Eric, she was once bitten and twice shy when it came to that sort of thing.

The weeks started to go quickly as they developed a sort of routine. She and Alejandro would go out Friday nights, either to a restaurant or someplace on the ranch to eat a picnic-style meal. Then Savannah would come over Saturday and Sunday afternoon, providing that she'd finished all her homework.

Halloween came and went, with Clara making Savannah a wonderful Amelia Earhart costume, while Alejandro dressed as a cowboy and Charity was a doctor. Yes, everyone thought it was hilarious, especially Savannah.

Then winter set in and the chores decreased, with Papa and Clara turning their attention to projects they could finish inside, and Charity had to close the doors of her workshop instead of spreading out all around it like she wanted to. And nights out to restaurants turned into nights in front of Alejandro's fireplace, curled up together and talking, or watching movies, and trying to keep their hands to themselves.

They weren't always successful on that last part, but it helped to have Savannah around to keep them accountable. It was just so easy to get swept up in each other and everything that they were feeling. She was falling in love, something she thought would never happen for her again, and she spent her days vacillating between scared out of her mind and happier than she'd been in ages. She tried to keep her imagination reined in, but it was so easy to imagine what the future could be like if the three of them were able to find a happy ending in each other.

More time passed, and before Charity knew it, it was December. Christmas was right around the corner, and she was contemplating how to invite both Savannah and Alejandro over for the day. It shouldn't have been hard, but she found herself tripping over it several times, and instead somehow ended up inviting the two of them sledding about two hours north of the ranch.

It was a special sort of sledding area that was behind a museum, arranged around a couple of hills and a flat area that was used as a cross-country skiing sort of track. Charity hadn't been there in a couple years, but she remembered having a great time when she was there before. Also, they had some *really* delicious hot chocolate.

They arrived without incident, and Savannah was off like a shot with her brand-new sled. Charity couldn't exactly blame her for being eager to go; the young girl *had* just spent a little over two hours crammed into a car.

"I'll go after her," Charity said with a laugh. "You go stand in line for the hot chocolate. It's usually at least a fifteen-minute wait."

"That popular, huh?"

"Yeah, you'll see why."

"You haven't steered me wrong yet." At that he leaned slightly, just enough to press a kiss to the top of her head. That was enough to send warmth shooting through her despite the cold, and she flushed before running off.

It was exhilarating to chase after Savannah then follow

her down the hill in their circle sleds. She didn't have to worry about either of them being hurt by a sudden stop at the bottom, because there were dozens and dozens of hay bales all set up for people to crash into. None supplied by the Miller ranch, unfortunately.

When they both reached the bottom and readied for the climb back up, Savannah was almost vibrating with her excitement, cheeks red and panting slightly.

"I never knew snow could be so fun!" Savannah said, skittering up the stairs carved into the packed ice.

"You've never seen snow before?"

Savannah shook her head. "Not really. Like, once when I was a baby, it apparently snowed while Dad and Mom were driving through Missouri for something, but I was too young to remember it."

"Why didn't you say so before?"

"Didn't I?" Savannah actually paused for a moment, a considering look on her face. "Oh, I guess I was so excited that I just forgot. Dad and I spent a lot of time online shopping for winter clothes. I've never owned snow boots or a coat this thick before, aren't they nice?!"

Charity took in her galaxy-themed coat and her shooting star boots with rainbows across the toes. They were definitely Savannah. "They look fantastic."

"Yeah! We might have gotten a few more pairs than we need since this is so far away, but I uh, I guess we got carried away. Dad says he hasn't played in the snow since before I was born."

"That's a long time," Charity agreed.

"Exactly. I'm going to be eleven in January. That's more than a decade."

"It *is*."

Finally, they reached the top of the hill and Charity was huffing n' puffing a bit more than she would have liked to be. But that embarrassment faded as Alejandro sauntered up to them, handing her and Savannah drinks from one of his hands and holding his own in the other. Charity didn't understand how he could hold two Styrofoam cups in one hand, even if they were so much bigger than hers.

"Wow, this *is* good!" Savannah gasped once she took her first sip. "Why is this so good? It's just hot chocolate."

"It's that good because they don't make it from powder here. It's their own recipe."

"...you can make hot chocolate not from powder?"

"Yup."

"*Amazing*," Savannah said before gulping down more.

Charity finally allowed herself a drink—she always had to let it cool a bit—and the rich, buttery smoothness of it slid over her tongue. *Delicious.*

"I have to admit, I didn't know that hot chocolate could be made from anything other than powder either," Alejandro said quietly.

"Well, maybe there is cocoa powder in it, but that's not the only thing. I'm not exactly super clear on the recipe, I just know it's not those little packets you get from the store."

"That makes sense."

She nodded, and the three of them just watched everyone else around them having fun and sliding down the hill as they sipped at their drinks. If anyone else were looking at their little group, they probably would have thought that they were a real family.

And Charity *felt* like they were a real family. It was just so easy to see, their little trio drinking delicious treats together on a mini getaway just for them. And that very idea made her feel so *good*. She was warm and satisfied in a way she wasn't used to. She didn't feel like her only solace was with the horses or in her workshop.

"Alright, give me your empty cups," she said when everyone was done. "I'll go toss them while the two of you go down the hill." Her plan was that if she and Alejandro traded off trips with Savannah, they just might have a fighting chance to last as long as she did. She supposed they could let the young girl go alone a couple of times, but that seemed too risky for her. Maybe she was just paranoid, but who knew what could happen when a minor was left unsupervised for even a few minutes when they were two hours away from her home.

"Yay! You ready, Dad?"

"About as ready as I'll ever be."

The two went off and *goodness,* as if that wasn't the most adorable thing ever. Charity watched them all the way down to the bottom, where Alejandro definitely collided with some hay bales much more dramatically than she or Savannah did.

It was as the two were laughing and clambering back up that her phone rang loudly from her pocket. No doubt Cass to check in and gloat over the fact that she was the one who gave Charity the sledding idea in the first place.

She answered it without looking, too busy watching Alejandro slip and slide and Savannah trying to help him by shoving him forward, and the two just tumbled together into the snow, laughing and shrieking.

"Hello?" she asked lazily, prepared for another round of banter with her sibling.

"My lawyer's last letter to you was marked 'Return to Sender.' You wanna tell me what that's about?"

Suddenly the world dropped out from under her feet, her

body going cold in a way the environment hadn't. That voice was familiar to her, down to the deepest, darkest part of her soul, but it was also a voice she'd never wanted to hear again.

"Eric," she said flatly, her mind spinning. What was he doing? Why was he calling her? She'd blocked his number, even had her lawyer put it into the court agreement that he wouldn't blow up her phone anymore, and yet he was right in her ear, snide and biting and oh, so superior.

"So, I hear from a couple of my friends that you've been seeing someone. Running around the town with some doctor wetb—"

"You're not supposed to contact me," she said sharply, her temper rising. "Move on, Eric. Leave me alone."

"Leave you alone? You took up nearly ten years of my prime, Charity. You *owe* me! And you have so much, but you're so greedy about it, you and your entire family. And don't think it's just coming from me. My lawyer—"

"If your lawyer *really* thinks something, then have him contact my lawyer like he's supposed to. You're breaking our agreement by harassing me, Eric. So stop it, before I stop being so generous with how much I've been willing to pay out for you to leave me alone."

"*Generous!* You think you're *generous?* You're delusional, Charity. Just some spoiled, small-town little girl who—"

"Who is that?" Alejandro asked sharply.

Charity nearly jumped out of her skin, yelping and looking to the bundled-up doctor. She hadn't even realized that the two had climbed up the hill. When had that happened?

"Is that him? The doctor you've duped into dating you? Has he realized how utterly useless you are yet? Or maybe he's in the closet. It would explain why he'd go after a woman who always acts like a—"

"May I have the phone, please?" Alejandro continued, hand extended.

It wasn't a demand. It wasn't even forceful. But Charity found herself locked into his gaze, his pull, and handed it over.

"Hello," Alejandro said more than asked. Charity heard a flurry of angry sentences, but he just stood there, impassive. "Yes, those were certainly words that you said, but not a lot of sense. Let me enlighten you on the situation, since you seem to have misunderstood exactly what is going on.

"You will never contact Charity again. I'm sure you're used to her giving you allowances because she is a generous, kind person. I will do no such thing. I'm a doctor, if you didn't know that. Have you ever had a doctor as an enemy? It's a complicated sort of thing. I have friends across the country, teachers, fellow students, people I met in residency. I have patients whose lives I saved that happen to be CEOs all the way down to owners of mechanic shops. If you insist on continuing to be the scum of the earth and inserting yourself into Charity's life, I won't hesitate to make your life miserable.

"And I can make it *so* miserable. Finding your job, getting you blacklisted, those are all easy things. There's so much more that can be done to a person, things that can ruin them and keep them up all night, with only a well-placed call to a private investigator, or even the IRS.

"So, if you want to avoid all that, hang up now, delete this number, and enroll yourself with a therapist. You certainly need it."

Charity stared at him with wide eyes, hardly believing

what she was hearing. But then Alejandro was handing her phone back to her, his expression completely serious.

"I don't think he's going to bother you again."

Her mouth opened. Her mouth closed. She swallowed and then tried again, but the shock was still layered throughout her. "I can't believe you just did that," she said eventually, wondering if she hit her head on the bottom of the hill and somehow was imagining everything.

"He was threatening you. I'm not going to let someone talk to anyone like that, but especially not the woman I love."

Charity *did* actually let out the tiniest gasp at that, and she felt her heart choose to skip a few beats. Alejandro looked to her like he was worried he'd upset her, and she didn't even think he understood what he'd said.

Naturally, it had to be Savannah who piped up. "So you do finally admit that you love Charity?"

"What?" Alejandro's eyes went wide, and he finally seemed to realize exactly what had left his mouth. Color rose on his cheeks even more than what was caused by the bite of the crisp cold air, and he looked like he wanted to backtrack.

She couldn't blame him. They'd only been dating for barely two months. That was awfully fast to drop the "L" bomb. If he retracted it, sure, it would hurt, but she wouldn't blame him.

"I said—" Savannah started to repeat herself before Alejandro interrupted.

"I heard what you said. I just..." But he didn't retract it. Instead, he took a deep breath and spoke. "Yes. I do love Charity. Very much so. Even if it seems crazy."

What!?

Charity stared at him, the world dropping away for the second time in just a few minutes, and all she could do was stare. He... he loved her? Like *loved* her, loved her? Alejandro wasn't the type to say what he didn't mean.

"Y-you love me?"

"I do. And I didn't say anything all this time because I was afraid it was too early, or it would scare you off, but I love you, Charity. You're the best thing that's happened to us in a long, long time. And you don't have to say it now, but I just want—"

"*Iloveyoutoo!*" she blurted, so fast that the words were practically mush in her mouth. Oh geez, that wasn't discernable to anybody. Taking a shaky breath herself, just like Alejandro, she forced herself to slow down. "I love you too. Very much. And it's scary, but I do. *So* much so."

He took a step towards her and she took a step towards him, feeling as drawn to him as she always did. Two magnets, opposites and yet made of the same thing, always calling to each other.

"I suppose it's not the strangest thing to say that I love my girlfriend."

"Girlfriend, huh? So we're putting labels on this then?" she whispered, feeling so charged from the moment that she was sure she could actually power her phone.

"Yeah," he rumbled, his voice dropping again in a way that made her shiver. "If you want to."

"Oh, I do, very much so."

"Glad to hear we're on the same page."

They were barely a breath away from each other, their gazes locked. She could almost feel his heartbeat through the air, intense and visceral.

"*Eeew!*" Savannah squealed from beside them. "Are you two gonna *kiss*?!?" She covered her face and recoiled, but when Charity glanced at her, the young girl was peeking out between a couple of her fingers, giggling ever so slightly.

"Yeah, we are," she said before going up onto her toes and planting one on Alejandro's awaiting face.

And it was just as wonderful as every kiss, just as full of all the nice things that she could ever want. She was so happy that she could burst, and wouldn't that be a way to go. It was still early, and there was still so much that could go wrong, but she really had a family right in her grasp. One of her own to add to everything that she already had. She'd always been meant to be a mom, she'd felt that in her bones since she was just fourteen, but for the first time in her life, she actually had a real chance to be one.

And she couldn't be more grateful for it.

EPILOGUE: CHARITY

A Year and a Half Later

Charity

Charity was in the middle of changing out the drive belt of Papa's riding lawn mower when her phone rang. Considering that Eric really hadn't called her after that moment on the sliding hill a year and a half ago, she didn't have to worry about someone unwanted being on the other end.

Life had been good, to put it mildly. Amazing, perfect, incredible even. She and Alejandro had been dating for nearly two years and were going exactly at the pace that they needed to.

Sure, there were some folks who kept asking when a ring was going to happen, but neither she nor Alejandro were in a rush. They were adults, and both realized that they had a lot of issues to work through, her with her distrust and him with his grief. But they worked *together*, going through the rough patches, the harder parts, and coming out on the other side a little wiser and a little more healed. There was no timeline for their love, and without that pressure, the three of them were able to build and grow their family however they wanted. They were all growing together, and it was everything she could ever ask for.

But still, with how good her life was going, when she wiped off her hands and hit to answer the call, she didn't expect the sound of sobbing to fill her ears.

"Charity," Savannah's voice barreled through the line, thick with tears and snot. "I think I'm dying. Please, come help me. I don't know what to do!"

"*Savannah*," Charity answered sharply, jumping to her feet. "That's not a funny joke."

She and the young girl had gotten even closer in the year and a half that had passed, even with the young girl landing solidly in the preteen stage of life where an attitude started to slip in. Somewhere along the line, she'd also developed a love of practical jokes and occasionally went over the line. Charity and Alejandro had both been working on teaching her that the best pranks were ones that hurt no one, but with how smart Savannah was, sometimes her tricks came across as more dastardly than hilarious.

"I'm not joking, Charity! Please, please come help me. I don't wanna *die*."

That... that didn't sound like a joke. At all. Sure, Savannah sometimes pointed out people's flaws, or made jokes that weren't jokes, but she didn't claim death. Especially not with what happened to her mother.

"Honey, do I need to call an ambulance? Or your father?"

"*No!* Don't call Dad! Just get here, please! My stomach has sharp, stabbing pains."

Sharp pain!? "I'll be there as quick as I can. It's gonna be alright, okay, Savannah?"

She groaned and then hung up, the line beeping in Charity's ear.

Charity was not a runner, not really, but she sprinted over to her truck and sped all the way to Alejandro's house. Either no cop saw her, or they knew she wasn't one to speed unless she had a good reason, because no one stopped her. She didn't even bother to lock her car, just rushing straight towards the door as fast as she could.

Her hands shook as she yanked her keys out, unlocking the door and bursting inside.

"Savannah! Savannah, where are you?"

"I'm in the bathroom upstairs," came the weak call.

More running, and then Charity was exploding into the room to see Savannah huddled on the ground, a pile of towels around her.

"Honey, what's wrong? Are you okay?"

"It *hurts*," she groaned, holding her abdomen.

There were tear tracks down her face, and Charity's heart squeezed so hard that it almost popped. She rushed over to the girl's side.

"And there's so much blood, Charity. I'm bleeding and I don't know why, and it's *everywhere!*"

At that she made a gesture to the toilet and, yeah, there was definitely blood on the seat.

With the evidence all laid out before her, Charity suddenly knew what was going on. It was both a relief and a bit of a shock.

"Savannah, love, has anyone ever told you what a period is?"

The girl sniffled, wiping at her cheeks as her eyes darted back and forth. "I... I think so. It's something to do with how women make babies?"

"Yes, that's very good. You see, when a girl starts to hit puberty, her reproductive system starts to practice things for later."

"Practice how?"

If it were anyone else, she might have gone with a flurried, less detailed explanation. But this was Savannah, who liked to read medical textbooks for fun. So Charity explained it in more detail. But still how a super smart pre-teen could understand.

At the end of her mini anatomy lesson, Charity added, "And it's nothing to be ashamed of. It's perfectly natural."

"But Charity, I'm bleeding from, uh, from down there."

"Yes, you are."

Sure, it was a strange conversation to have. Maybe even a little uncomfortable too. But there was also something somehow sweet about it. It was a special, tender moment usually shared between mothers and daughters. And while Charity wasn't Savannah's biological mother, she was the one who was there, helping the little girl understand her body as she became not so little.

"And I've got these, uh, cramp things too?"

"Yes, you do."

"So... does that mean I've got my period too?"

"Yes, Savannah. You have your period. It can be uncomfy and annoying, but there's nothing wrong with it. And if anyone tells you it's gross or tries to make it sound like it's something bad, they don't know what they're talking about."

"A lot of people don't react well to natural bodily functions. Which is silly."

"Exactly, it's silly."

When Savannah finally raised her head to look at Charity, the relief was evident across her features. Charity just wanted to snatch her up and hug her for just about forever, but maybe she would wait until the girl washed up and put pants on.

"But... you said this stuff is for women. I'm not a woman, not really. I just turned twelve a few months ago."

"Oh, I know, I know. You're still a girl, don't worry. But like I said, your body is practicing. It's learning how it needs to do what it wants to do for when you *are* grown up. You're entering puberty, honey, which can be scary, but is perfectly natural."

"O...okay. This all... this all doesn't sound very fun, to be honest."

At that Charity had to laugh, pulling the girl's upper half into a quick hug. "It's not most of the time, but it doesn't have to be miserable. How about you wash off with a shower, then take a good, long soak in a hot bath while I go to the store and get you some supplies."

"Supplies? What kind of supplies?"

"Well, feminine products for one. Has anyone ever taught you how to use a pad?"

Savannah shook her head solemnly.

"Right, well a couple different types of those, and then some chocolate cake and steak. Goodness knows when I'm in the thick of it, red meat and sugar always make me feel miles better."

"O-okay. And you're sure I'll be fine?"

"Yes. I promise it."

The girl nodded and wiped her face once more, squaring

her shoulders with a determination that never failed to make Charity's heart go soft and squishy.

"Charity?"

"Yeah, honey?"

"Why didn't anyone tell me about this?"

"I'm not sure. Aren't you supposed to have health class?"

"Yeah, but not until next year, in eighth grade."

"Ah, okay. Seems like they'd do it a little earlier, seeing as how some girls get their periods as early as nine or ten."

"This is *awful*. I'm glad I didn't have this when I was ten."

"Me too."

"But why didn't my dad tell me? He's a doctor?"

There was just the thinnest bit of hurt there, and *goodness*, it made Charity want to grab a sword and defend Savannah like an ancient princess. "That question has a complicated answer, sweetheart. I don't claim to speak for him, but a big part of it is probably just that he's a man. He probably didn't really think about it. But also, you're his little girl, his baby, and the thought of you being on your way to being a woman and not needing him anymore was something he *probably* wanted to avoid."

"But I'm always gonna need my dad! Even when I'm grown up!"

"Haha, that very well may be true, but it's different. He's your parent and he wants to watch you grow up and succeed, but also, maybe he's a little scared of when you move on like you're supposed to and live your own life."

"...oh. I... I think I understand. It's been just him and me so long. But he has you now..." There was that flicker of uncertainty again. "...right?"

"Right. Exactly. *Both* of you have me. So why don't you start with that washing up while I go grab our supplies."

"Okay."

"Good girl. I'll see you soon. And don't worry about cleaning up the mess. I'll take care of it while you take it easy today. You only get your first period once."

PERPHAPS IT WAS unusual for Charity to take pride in the fact that she was an excellent first-period fairy, but after going through it with herself, Cass, Clara and Cici, she'd gotten plenty of practice in. She was well aware that most folks had a mother to walk them through the process, but that hadn't been in the cards for her family.

She remembered how overwhelmed she'd been the first time, standing in the feminine hygiene aisle and looking at the seemingly endless amount of supplies. But she'd learned since, and helped her siblings learn, and now she was going to help Savannah too.

Was... was this what it was like to be a mother? It felt like it. And that feeling made her feel so full of love that if she didn't get a hold of herself, it was going to start to leak out of her eyes as tears.

Savannah was growing up. She was becoming an intelligent, unstoppable woman, and Charity had the honor of seeing it happen. How absolutely *wild*.

So yeah, maybe she went overboard and bought far more chocolate than any twelve-year-old needed, but who ever heard of too many sweets for a period? Not Charity. She also loaded up with iron and vitamin E supplements, remembering how Cici struggled with anemia every time her cycle came around. And then headache meds, medicine for cramps, some warm, soothing tea, and then a broad range of pads and panty liners.

She was well aware that people were giving her strange looks for her overflowing cart, but she didn't care. Being there for such a big milestone in Savannah's life was a gift, and one she wasn't going to take for granted.

It didn't take her overly long to get back home, and when she did, Savannah was still in the tub. So, Charity went about baking a cake in the kitchen, although she did use a box mix which no doubt would have horrified Clara.

Oh well, it was better than nothing, especially when Charity put an extra thick layer of cream cheese frosting on it.

The cake was on the counter and cooling by the time Savannah came down in her PJs, which had given Charity enough time to plug in a heating pad and brown the steaks. With a warm, soft hug, she assured the girl everything was going to be alright, then settled her in the bathroom once more before explaining the hygiene options and how to use them.

Savannah blushed several times, but Charity just acted like it was the most casual thing in the world. That seemed to help because, after about ten minutes, Savannah nodded and said she was okay to see what worked for her.

And then she'd hugged Charity again, clinging to her like the cowgirl was the last buoy in a choppy sea.

"I don't know what I would do without you. Dad's a doctor, but I don't think he'd know about all these, and how different they are."

"Probably not. But that's why we all work so well together, right? We pick up the slack for each other."

Savannah nodded, pressing her face against Charity's

shoulder. She'd grown again and was almost equal height with Charity.

"Please don't leave us, Charity. You're the best mom I've ever had."

Oh, oh *wow*. Savannah certainly knew exactly what to say to make Charity's emotions go into upheaval. "And you're the best daughter I could ever ask for. And I'm not going to leave you—or at least I have no plans too. You're stuck with me."

"Promise?"

"Promise."

She cheered at that, so Charity left her to figure out what felt best for her, setting the steaks out to rest and putting some of the chocolates in the fridge and others in the freezer. She found some tortilla chips in the cupboard along with some of the canned salsas left over from the most recent corn festival, then set some sodas in the fridge to chill.

Sure, it was a bit over the top, and certainly not a healthy thing to do *every* period. But for the first one, there was nothing wrong with a little indulgence.

When Savannah appeared again, she was shifting back and forth uncomfortably. Charity invited her to sit on the couch and swaddled the girl with blankets, bringing her the heating pad as well, then putting a fan on her in case her face got overheated like Clara's always did.

After that, the young girl seemed to relax as they both ate some steak and left-over potatoes in the fridge, then she downed some medicine for cramp relief. They put on one of her favorite movies, a trilogy about elves and orcs and the end of their world, then just chilled out. Occasionally Savannah would pause the movie to ask a question about puberty, her period specifically, or other things that might be coming, and

Charity did her best to always answer them as nonchalantly as she could.

It was sometime just after six when Alejandro walked in, hanging his keys and calling out that he was home. He was walking into the living room a moment later and stopped short when he saw Charity there and his daughter almost buried in blankets with a truly impressive amount of junk food around them.

"Um, I'm sorry... did I forget about a date or something?"

He looked so concerned for a moment that Charity couldn't help but bark out a laugh. However, when that concern only grew, she sobered and cleared her throat.

"Savannah, do you want to tell your dad something?"

Savannah didn't reply right away, her brow furrowing in a perfect mirror of her father while she considered what she wanted to say, if she actually wanted to say anything at all. Charity, who wouldn't force the issue either way, just sat back and listened.

"I'm a woman now," Savannah said with a nod of her head. "Or... at least on my way to being one. So, you have to be nice to me."

It shouldn't have been so adorable to see Alejandro's expression grow even more confused. Men. She wondered what life was like for them sometimes.

Turning her head to look at him over Savannah, she gave him a meaningful look. He still stared, dumbfounded for several moments before she finally saw it click.

"Oh. *Oh.* That's, uh, that's a big deal, Savannah. How are you feeling?"

"Better now. Charity got me pain medicine and stuff I needed. We also ate a ton of chocolate."

Charity hadn't been entirely certain of how Alejandro

would respond, but she certainly wasn't expecting for his slightly incredulous expression to shift into something that seemed slightly hurt. "Why did you call Charity and not me? You know you can always trust me with any health stuff, right *miha*? I'm a doctor, after all."

"*Daaad*," she said with that particular tone that preteens and teenagers used because they know everything in the world and then some. "It was *embarrassing* and you're a guy. Besides, I knew I could trust Charity to come and take care of me. She's smart and would know what was wrong, but also wouldn't freak out.

"And I was right, you know. She knew a lot of stuff that I bet you wouldn't have. And that's the whole point of you dating, right? You pick up the slack for each other."

Hearing her words out of Savannah's mouth did something to Charity, and goodness if her eyes weren't growing misty at that. When her gaze returned to Alejandro, she saw that he looked equally touched.

"You really feel that way about Charity?"

"Of course," was Savannah's blithe reply. "Don't you?"

Their eyes locked, and the amount of depth in Alejandro's nearly stole all of Charity's breath away. It shouldn't be possible to see so much in just a simple gaze, but she absolutely did. It was overwhelming, but in the best way possible.

"Yes, yes of course I do." He took a shuddering breath, and wouldn't it be something if the two adults broke into tears while the young girl on her period maintained her cool? "Could, uh, could you two just wait here a minute?"

Savannah shifted under her blankets. "Does it honestly look like I'm equipped to go anywhere?"

"Fair point. I'll be right back."

Without another word, he bolted up the stairs and out of

sight. Charity and Savannah exchanged glances at the sudden escape.

"That was weird, even for my dad."

"It was, but I'm sure he has his reasons."

"Yeah, he usually does."

There were a couple minutes of listening to him frantically stomp around upstairs, quite dramatically, and then he was thundering down the stairs. Charity had never really seen Alejandro rush quite like that, and her curiosity began to peak with every passing moment.

"Uh, Charity, could you come here for a moment?"

"Why?" she said whining, but mostly just to get a rise out of him. He looked so intense that she really couldn't help it. What was going on in that handsome head of his? His hands were empty, so it wasn't like he'd brought anything down from his sudden escape to the upper floors of the house.

"Just uh, do it. Please?"

"Well, since you're asking so nicely."

She did indeed get up, although she paused to wipe her face. Once she was sure she didn't have any frosting or crumbs there, she crossed to him with what she knew was an expectant look on her face.

"Look, if you're still mad that she called me and not you—"

But he just shook his head. "No. Nothing like that. Just... just let me catch my breath."

"Hah, don't worry, I'm used to having that effect on people." She pantomimed tossing her hair over her shoulder haughtily and that seemed to break whatever tension was coiling in Alejandro. Of course, when he relaxed, she expected a hug or a kiss from him. The last thing she'd anticipated was for him to suddenly kneel in front of her, pulling a small black box from his pocket.

Oh my goodness, was he about to do what Charity thought he was going to do!?

"Charity Miller, you are one of the most beautiful, intelligent, and fiercely loving women that I have ever met. I love you with all of my heart and soul.

"I was hardly living before you, and Savannah carried me through every day. But now, I have things to live for. Hopes and dreams. I don't wake up and dread that I have to survive through another day, and I owe that all to you.

"I know I have a lot still to do. I know that I still struggle with grief and giving myself permission to feel all the things I feel, but I know without a shadow of a doubt that I want to keep working, keep getting better. And I want to get better with *you.*

"So, Miss Charity Miller, will you do me the honor of being my wife?"

With every word out of his mouth, her eyes began to burn and her heart beat faster and faster. By the time he asked the question, she swore her heart was going to leap right up and out of her chest.

"*Yes,*" she said, barely able to get the words out. All of her own feelings, her own dreams swirled within her, and she knew she was shaking as he slid the ring onto her hand. "Yes, Alejandro, I love you more than I've ever loved anyone in my life."

The ring sparkled on her finger, reminding her of the stars that glittered on that first night they'd spent out on the hiking trail. She was staring at it, almost unbelieving that it was actually there, when Alejandro practically jumped to his feet and kissed her silly.

She sighed into it, leaning against him like she was melting, her arms wrapping around his neck. And she held him just like that, lips pressed against each other, sharing a moment that would define the rest of their lives.

They didn't part until they heard Savannah clear her throat, and when they did, Charity saw the young woman had indeed pushed herself out of her cushions to stand on the couch, her phone in her hand.

"You guys are so lucky I kept my head enough to record that," she said with a crooked grin that looked so much like her father it was uncanny.

"That we are," Alejandro said with a booming laugh. "At least one of us kept our head."

But then the moment really started to catch up with Charity, and she gave the man a look. "Wait, did you just propose to me because your daughter got her period?" That couldn't be it, but the timing...

He laughed again, tilting his head back. It was such an open, relieved sound that she found herself echoing it.

"I already had the ring on hand, so I was already thinking about it. But, like usual, I was letting fear dissuade me from taking the leap."

"And what about this mildly traumatic experience made you man up?" Savannah asked, sinking back on the couch. Despite her word choice, she was grinning from ear to ear and swiping through her phone, no doubt reviewing all the pictures and recordings she'd taken of the moment.

"It's because this made it clear that you're meant to be in our lives, Charity. That you're better for us than I could have ever imagined and that I love you with all of my heart. I know, if Tirza could talk to us, she would be so happy that you're here to take care of her daughter."

Well, when he put it like *that.*

"I love you too, Alejandro. More than I ever thought was possible."

"Charity?"

"Yes, Alejandro?"

"I want to kiss you again."

"Then do it. I am your fiancée, after all."

"Ugh, are you two gonna keep being so *gross*?"

"Oh yeah," Alejandro answered as his arms encircled Charity's waist. "*So* gross. For the rest of your lives."

"Ugh. You're lucky I like the two of you."

"I'm *incredibly* lucky," Alejandro replied, his voice low. But Charity knew he was talking to her more than his daughter. "And I'm never going to forget it."

And with that, they kissed again, her heart soaring right next to his. They were going to be *married.* Against all the odds, against everything stacked against them, they'd made it.

They had a whole life ahead of them, but for once, Charity wasn't afraid of it.

EPILOGUE: ALEJANDRO

Alejandro

"Are you sure you want to do this?" Charity asked nervously, fidgeting with the flowers in her lap.

"We already flew here, rented a car, and drove the rest of the way. It'd be silly to turn around now."

"But we could, if you wanted to. You don't have to—"

He reached over, settling his large hand over her smaller one. "It's fine, Charity. I want this. I promise. And so does Savannah."

He watched his fiancé's gaze flick back to Savannah, who nodded enthusiastically from the back seat.

"Alright. Okay. I just, uh, I'm ready then. If you're sure."

"I absolutely am."

She nodded, licking her lips, and then she was getting out of their rented car. Alejandro followed suit, coming around the other side so both of his loves could link their arms through his.

It was together that they walked up the neatly cobblestoned path to a grassy knoll, his fiancée, his daughter, and so many memories between them. They walked in silence, save for the rustling of the bouquet, and it wasn't until several minutes later that they reached their destination.

A place achingly familiar to him. A place where he used to come and sob, used to curse God and ask him how he could ever take away the best part of his life. But now, as they approached Tirza's grave, he felt something else entirely.

"Hello, love," he murmured, letting go of Charity and Savannah to kneel by her headstone. "I'm sorry it's been so long since I last visited. But I wanted to introduce you to someone."

He reached out his hand for Charity, and she came and knelt beside him, laying the bouquet of flowers on the ground.

"Hello there, Tirza. It's nice to finally meet you. Your daughter is amazing. Alejandro's not bad either."

Alejandro chuckled at that. "See? I told you I found someone to keep me in line." The wind rustled, but of course there was no answer. That wasn't how it worked. But still, Alejandro had wanted to pay his respects, and also to show his first beloved that he had kept his promise to her. Finally, after far too many years, he'd opened his heart and let himself love again.

"I know the best thing would be if you were still here," Charity continued, "but I promise I'll take care of them with everything I have. I love them, more than I ever thought possible, and I'll protect them with my life. Forever."

Alejandro practically glowed at the words, because he

knew that Charity absolutely meant them. She didn't say things that she didn't mean.

"So, I hope I have your blessing. Alejandro told me that you made him promise not to shut himself off from moving along, and I can't thank you enough for that blessing. He and Savannah complete me. They're my family, through and through."

She looked to Alejandro and gave him a nod, her hand squeezing his. That gave him the strength to say what he needed, the words that had been building up in his soul. "I love you, Tirza, and I always will. I was so hurt for so long, and sure that there couldn't be life without you, so for years I couldn't come see you here. It hurt too much. But I'm healing now.

"I still falter, and I still get stuck sometimes. You know how stubborn I can be. You were always so much better at this than me. But I'm trying. Every day I'm trying because I do love Charity with all of my heart.

"I didn't know that I could love her and also you, but I absolutely do. So, thank you, Tirza, for everything. All of it. I will carry you with me for the rest of my life, and I can't wait for all of us to meet when our time comes."

Then it was his turn to look to Savannah, who was staring at the grave with a quizzical expression.

"She's not really there," the young girl said, brows furrowed. "I don't understand the point of this exercise."

That pricked at Alejandro, making his resolution crumple, but then Charity was reaching out with her hand, fingers wiggling for Savannah to take her hand. His daughter did, coming closer to kneel next to the cowgirl.

"No, she's not literally there, but that doesn't mean she's not all around us."

"What do you mean?"

"You know how your mom is in heaven, right?" A nod. "Well, heaven isn't some place in the sky. It exists around us, through us, everywhere. Sometimes it's in that feeling you get when you go out to feed the horses right after it's rained. Sometimes it's when you open a book for the first time, ready to devour someone else's ideas.

"And right now, heaven is right here, and if you open yourself to it, you just might feel your mother here."

"Really?"

Charity nodded. "Really. Heaven isn't a fixed coordinate on the map. It's there, if you just let yourself reach for it."

Savannah closed her eyes, saying nothing for several long beats, but when she did speak, shivers went down Alejandro's back.

"I didn't know you that well, Mom. I've got these flashes of memories, but that's it. Sometimes I feel like I'm a bad daughter because I know so little about you."

Alejandro opened his mouth to protest, to assure Savannah that she was wonderful in every way, but Charity squeezed his hand and gave him a slight shake of her head.

"But as I get older, I feel like I keep finding more pieces of you. I read the letters you wrote me and tucked into the baby journal. I know you wanted to give them to me as I grew up, and even though you're not here to physically do it, it was like you were there anyway.

"I see you in my face, sometimes. I see you in the way Dad talks about the recipes you taught him. And I see you every time I think how you sent Charity to us.

"Because that was you, I know it was. I can feel it down to my toes. So, I just wanted to say thank you, for giving me a mom since it couldn't be you. I'll never forget that. I promise."

It was so sweet, so honest, that Alejandro didn't even try to fight the tears in his eyes. He had no idea that his daughter had felt that way, but it touched him to his core.

They stayed there for several long moments, the seconds heavy but not exhausting. There was so much left to say, so much left to tell, but he wasn't going to avoid the spot anymore. Once a year, they would take a trip to San Diego to pay their respects.

Eventually, when they were ready to stand, Savannah and Charity took his arms again.

"Are you alright?" Charity asked, her voice layered with so much love and concern that it was dizzying.

"I am now."

"It's about time," Savannah replied with her trademark grin, managing to get a slight chuckle from all of them.

And it was together that they walked down the hill and into their future, together.

As a family.

~

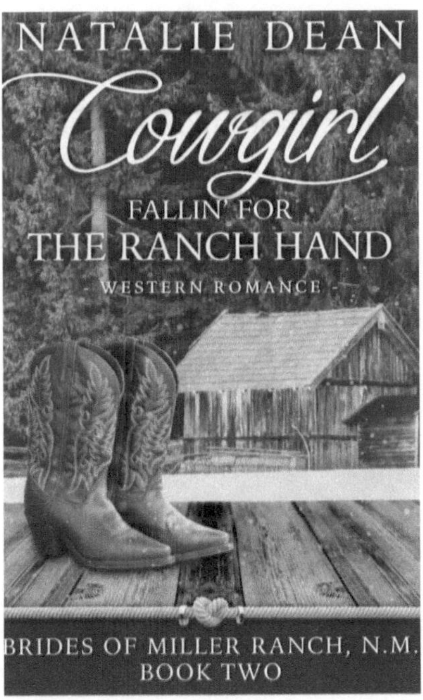

HELLO READERS! I hope you enjoyed Chasity and Alejandro's love story. I kind of secretly included one of my favorite kinds of people in this book. Autistic kiddos! My son is on the spectrum and so is Savannah in this book. So I hope you enjoyed that.

Next up is Cassidy and Mick's sweet romance. Cassidy can't pull her load around the ranch at the moment, so they decide to hire someone to help. He's a drifter and doesn't plan on staying too long. But you know how that goes in love stories...

You can find Cassidy and Mick's love story on all major retailers. But of course, as previously mentioned, it sure would be great if you could support my small bookstore. Scan the QR code below (might be on the next page, depending on the book format) to be taken to Cowgirl Fallin' for the Ranch

Hand at Natalie Dean Books. If scanning QR codes isn't your thing, you can find my store here: nataliedeanbooks.com Just look under the Miller stories tab for Brides of Miller Ranch, N.M., and you should be able to find this book.

ABOUT THE AUTHOR

Born and raised in a small coastal town in the south, I was raised to treasure family and love the Lord. I'm a dedicated homeschooling mom who loves to travel and spend time with my growing-up-too-fast son.

When I'm not busy writing or running my business, you can find me cleaning house, cooking dinner, feeding our three rescue cats, trying to make learning fun and coaxing my son to pick up his toys. On less busy days, you may also find me paddling down a spring run in Florida, hiking a mountain trail in Georgia (on the rare vacation to the mountains), or enjoying a book.

If you love Natalie Dean books, you can be notified of new releases by signing up to my newsletter at nataliedeanau thor.com, where you will also receive two free short stories for signing up. Just click on the "Free Books" tab at the top and you'll be on your way!

Also, as previously mentioned, I've opened my own online bookstore and I'd love your support! As of June 2024, I'm selling my ebooks at Natalie Dean Books. By late summer or fall 2024, I should have audiobooks, regular paperbacks, large print paperbacks, dyslexic print paperbacks and signed paperbacks all available. At the request of my loyal readers, I'll also be adding merchandise, such as glasses, cups, magnets and more. So come check out my small mom-owned author business at nataliedeanbooks.com.

You can also scan the QR code below to be taken to the home page of Natalie Dean Books.

facebook.com/nataliedeanromance